Medusa's Lair

Medusa's Lair

A Chic Sparks—Fish House Gang Novel

KENNETH L. FUNDERBURK

ARCHWAY
PUBLISHING

Scripture taken from the King James Version of the Bible.

This is a work of fiction. All of the characters, names, incidents, organizations, and dialogue in this novel are either the products of the author's imagination or are used fictitiously.

Archway Publishing books may be ordered through booksellers or by contacting:

Archway Publishing
1663 Liberty Drive
Bloomington, IN 47403
www.archwaypublishing.com
1 (888) 242-5904

ISBN: 978-1-4808-5017-0 (sc)
ISBN: 978-1-4808-5018-7 (e)

Library of Congress Control Number: 2017911225

Print information available on the last page.

Archway Publishing rev. date: 7/24/2017

Chapter

1

Chic Sparks is a practicing clinical psychologist in Pensacola, Florida, who also acts as a profiler for the sheriff and other law enforcement departments in the area. Chic and his love, Suzy, were on their way home after his performance at the River Center in Columbus, Georgia. Chic performed the tenor aria in Handel's *Messiah* along with a combined choir of Schwob Conservatory's Choral Union and Auburn University's Chamber Choir. The choirs were accompanied by the Columbus Symphony Orchestra directed by George Del Gobbo. The cold weather and drizzle of rain forced them to close the top on Suzy's red Mustang.

"You did a wonderful job tonight, Chic. As usual, you were the crowd's favorite. " Suzy grabbed Chic's hand and said, "You're always my favorite."

Chic, looking a little self-conscious, smiled and said, "Thanks." Chic reached over and gently took Suzy's shoulders, pulling her to his body.

"You know, this is one of my favorite places to perform. The combined choirs were marvelous. George Del Gobbo, the orchestra director, is great to work with. This place is really like home to me. My training days here at Fort Benning are still close to my heart."

"You can thank them, Chic, that you're the tough guy you are. Thank God for that, or I might be a dead chick." Suzy had a big grin.

They both knew the truth. Chic had managed to help save Suzy's life and repair her troubled heart. Suzy snuggled up a little closer to Chic as they traveled down 431 toward Pensacola in silence. Suzy looked up at Chic; he had a worried look on his face, and she could feel a little tenseness in his body.

"Okay, Chic, when you get that look, something's bothering you. What's up?"

"I'm just concentrating on my driving, that's all."

"No, you're pondering something, and I can tell it's not making you happy. Now tell mama and get it off your chest."

"Well, I really wasn't going to break the spell about the wonderful time I had performing tonight, as well as the pleasure of your company, but as soon as we got in the car, I had this foreboding come over me. Frankly, it takes me a little thought to focus on the problem myself. You know that before you and I met, I performed Foust here in Columbus at the same River Center. At more or less the same time, the Ninja gang killed that couple in Pensacola, which eventually led to my getting into the case, essentially to help you. You were personally being threatened because the murders thought you had information, which you didn't have. If it had not been for that situation, I would probably have never met you. I hope you know that meeting you was the greatest day of my life."

Suzy leaned over and kissed Chic as carefully as she could without causing a wreck. This man had saved her life in many ways.

Suzy knew that Chic was too much of a man to bring up what actually got her involved accidentally in a murder case. Suzy had made the mistake of getting involved in a sexual threesome, two of whom had a connection to the Ninja gang. At the time of the threesome, a couple of gangsters broke in and managed to kill the other two, but she escaped with her life. She turned to Chic for help, and he freely gave it.

"I'm sorry that I sucked you into that mess, but I knew you were the only person who could save me," Suzy said. "So, why do you have that foreboding feeling?

"I can't explain it other than I'm reminded that the entire story of that crime spree is essentially still open. While we were able to eliminate the local gang, we were not able to identify the larger crime lords behind the local criminals. Then there's the issue with Ken Renfro, my good friend, who turned out to be the biggest crime boss in probably the Southeast. We don't know if he's alive. We only know he disappeared. So Ken or his gang represent a real threat to both of us."

"How was Ken able to hide his criminal connections from you, Chic? He had to be good to fool you, my love."

Chic chuckled. "Now, don't rub it in. For me, that was a personal disaster. A real trauma. Ken was my friend, and I'm certain he looked at me the same way. I had no clue of his activity until the very end. When we found out, he was able to totally disappear into the air. I'm certain the crime bosses, whoever they are, killed him. Their pattern was to kill all the adverse witnesses. But let's face it. It would be against logic to think that these criminals have simply forgotten about you and me."

Suzy turned a little pale at the thought of having to fight for her life once again. "If you're worried, Chic, then I'm petrified."

Chic pulled Suzy a little closer. "Don't worry. baby. I'll take care of you."

"Right now, there's nothing going on locally to give local law enforcement any reason to think Ken's gang is back in town. But that doesn't mean they have forgotten the misery I've caused them."

"So, my love, let us pray that your foreboding is simply an upset stomach." As Suzy snuggled up to Chic, she was thankful that this man was her protector, but then she knew that Chic's revelations were usually spot-on.

Chapter

2

Campeche Bank is located along the north-northwest shore of the Yucatan Peninsula in the Gulf of Mexico and is well known for nursing hurricanes. In the fall, three days is as long as it takes to form a named storm maintaining cyclonic winds and torrential rain. It is a legendary area where millions of years ago the dinosaurs met their end when a meteorite crashed into the Gulf of Mexico. The falling star created absolute darkness upon impact with the Earth. The surviving large mammals would never again see the light of day.

Every careful sailor, versed in the history of the Gulf of Mexico, knows that September through November is that time of the year when hurricanes, forming off Cape Verde and the west coast of Africa, eventually deliver nature's wrath to the gulf and the eastern seaboard of North America. Likewise, on what may have begun as a fair-weather sail, the tempests can form quickly and intensely off Campeche Bank, destroying a slow boat before it safely crosses the gulf.

Nathan Corley, captain of *Heaven*, a reefer cargo ship, was eyeing the building storm as he paced back and forth on the bridge, barely able to control his rage. His plea to delay the shipment of shrimp and red snapper to a wholesale house in Key West, Florida, went unheeded. He did not want to be headed out into the Gulf of Mexico with a strong tropical depression surging right into him from the east. In fact, if he had anything to do with anything, he would have steamed straight for a safe anchorage instead of setting a course that would pin him down on the shallow Campeche Bank. Yet that's exactly what his boss, Echeneis, the proud and boastful owner of Echeneis Shipping Lines, insisted that he do.

Captain Corley glanced over at the VHF radio on the bridge, painfully aware of the poor guy screaming, "Mayday! Mayday!" over and over again. Then he gave his latitude/longitude.

"Poor sucker," Frank said. Corley's first mate shot him a grim smile. "Better him than us, I guess."

Corley coughed and took a swig of bottled water. "I suppose so," he said. "Just wish we could help. We're only five nautical miles to the west of his position."

Frank nodded. "But you know we can't stop to help."

"Yeah. I know. The poor bastard should have known better than to screw with the Campeche Bank in weather like this."

Just then, a brilliant fork of white-hot lightning ripped the sky off the starboard bow. "Looks like we're going to take a hit," Frank said.

Corley sighed. "Yeah, looks like it, don't it?"

"Frank," snarled Nathan, "I'm going to take one more shot at the home office. What possible excuse could they have for risking our lives and the ship in weather like this?"

Frank simply shook his head in disgust. He looked at the captain and could see the blood rising in his normally calm face—the kind of man who kept steady at the helm even in a storm.

The captain's conversation with the home office was short. He managed to get out of his mouth, "What the hell are you thinking? You're putting the boat and crew's lives at risk here." His face flashed another shade of red.

The captain turned to Frank. "So much for my due diligence. Tonight we'll find out the limits of our seamanship."

Captain Corley carried 185 pounds on his frame of five feet eleven inches. He looked like he came from English stock. Corley was a family man with two grown children and a wife who looked great for her age. You could tell he was an athlete by the way he handled himself. He kept his counsel within and was considered by his peers to be a man's man. While some sea captains qualified for the title only in their mother's eyes, Captain Corley was the real deal.

The ship was headed almost directly into the swells building to the north-northeast. Spray occasionally rose white at the tip of the bow when the vessel dipped deep into a trough. Corley guessed that the seas were already running at over fifteen feet, and the ship's anemometer registered wind gusts of over thirty knots. The robotic voice of NOAA Weather Radio cut in to issue a storm warning. The static on the VHF radio hissed and buzzed in the background. "Keep her steady, Frank," he said to his first mate. "Steady as she goes at twenty-five degrees magnetic." He smiled at his first mate, a gentle giant of a man who'd been a merchant mariner for more than thirty years.

"Aye, aye, sir!" Frank said.

Corley could see he was uneasy. "Somethin' on your mind, Frank?" he asked.

Frank shook his head and said, "Well, since you're kind enough to ask … the men have reported that they heard that we might be attacked tonight by the Zeta cartel because we have drugs on board."

"If we do, Frank, you and I could end up in a drug war. This is Zeta territory, and they would not look kindly on us hauling drugs out of Veracruz. That probably explains why the home office insisted we leave now, hoping the bad guys wouldn't attack us in bad weather in open seas."

Frank gave a little chuckle. "Well, Captain, if we've got drugs on board, then this is one crew of bad guys versus another crew of bad guys. This crew looks pretty tough to me, but I haven't seen any weapons. If the cartels are involved, you can bet they have weapons on board."

"Frank, one reason I had us wear our sidearms this trip was because these extra men we're carrying set me on edge. You do have your extra clips on you, I hope."

"Yes, Captain," I do.

Captain Corley grabbed the ship's intercom and summoned the ship's chief engineer to meet him in his stateroom immediately.

The chief engineer didn't like the idea of reporting to the captain like this, especially in bad weather and when he knew he had to remain on post to guard against any attacks. Begrudgingly, he fought his way up to the captain's stateroom where Captain Corley was waiting.

"Come on in, Chief." Corley was looking the chief in the eyes, holding his stare. The captain didn't like what he saw. "We have been hearing rumors about a pending attack by Zeta. What do you know about that?"

"Well, Captain, we heard some loose talk around the dock that we were in trouble and that Zeta was going to clean our plow. But you know that's a bunch of idle talk. Don't you worry about that, Captain Corley. These boys know how to take care of themselves in a fight. If those drug heads come near us, we'll blast them straight to hell."

"Chief, I can't imagine they would try anything in this storm, but who knows? Keep a close lookout. Do you know why they're after us? Do we have drugs on board or something else they might be after?"

"I don't know," said the crew chief. "I guess the Zeta cartel is out to prove something to the Sinaloa cartel."

"Well, are you a part of Sinaloa?" the captain asked.

"Hell no, Captain, but the rumor is that this ship is owned by the Sinaloa. I think Sinaloa wouldn't be shipping a product out of Veracruz unless they wanted to stir up some shit."

"Chief, I hope you don't take me for a fool. If Sinaloa put me and this ship in the lion's den, then they would have to have their team on board and in charge here. That means you and the crew are here to do battle. Now I've got to assume there are drugs on board, and you're in charge of security."

"If I were you, Captain, I would keep my opinions to myself," said the chief.

"You and I can settle this later, Chief. Right now, I need you to get your men in position to protect this cargo ship. Now get your ass out of here and get to work."

"Aye, aye, Captain," the chief spat out with a disrespectful smirk as he exited the navigation station.

As *Heaven* cleared the sea buoy out of Veracruz, Captain Jesús cursed under his breath and quickly loaded his five men into the RHIB. The boat was powered by two 250-horsepower Mercury engines blasting at maximum RPMs, headed directly in the direction of *Heaven*. This craft—a rigid, hard-bottom, inflated boat—was the favorite of all special ops teams the world over. It was a rotten day. The low-pressure system was rapidly intensifying into a hurricane. Their chance of success was low as far as capturing the cargo ship. They had a man on board *Heaven* who was going to throw them a boarding ladder once they neared the ship, but they were up against an experienced crew and bad weather.

Jesús knew *Heaven's* top speed was about thirteen knots. Taking into account the speed of the RHIB, he estimated he would catch *Heaven* about fifty to sixty miles out. Captain Jesús was certain there was a traitor on board *Heaven*. The plan was to pull off this caper at night, at dock—not on the high seas. The captain of *Heaven* must have gotten word about the heist and decided to leave early. Jesús's bosses were not only concerned with the $30 million in drugs in *Heaven's* hull, but they were also pissed because the Sinaloa cartel was using their port to ship drugs right under their collective noses. Risking his life and the lives of his crew meant less than nothing to those bastards at Zeta!

"Lock and load, boys. We're coming in hot," said Jesús. "Carlos, text our man on board to make ready with the ladder. He must release the ladder on two blinks from my flashlight."

The powerful RHIB, under the expertise of Jesús, behaved like a bucking bronco under the control of a master horseman. In the minds of these six mercenaries on board, they were in nirvana. The wind was blasting their bodies; they were riding at tremendous speed, tipping the tops of the angry waves. They were loaded for bear and pumped full of adrenalin, awaiting the impending bloodbath.

On cue, Jesús swung the RHIB sideways into the aft port side of *Heaven*. The men, dressed all in black, with goggles in place, mounted the waiting ladder, precise as gymnasts and perfectly synchronized.

By god, Jesús thought, *this is one hell of a tough bunch. I would follow these guys into hell.* Then it flashed into his mind. *There's a very real possibility that may happen this very day.*

———•———

Heaven's chief engineer began to make a deployment of his men as soon as he left the captain's quarters. By then it was dark. He retrieved the night goggles the men had brought along for such an occasion. He passed out the night goggles and then positioned his men fore and aft. They would be able to detect any approaching vessel and sound the alarm. Stationed on the starboard and port decks, the men were heavily armed and equipped with hands-free radios. They too were in black, enhanced with body armor and helmets. All ten were trained by US Army Special Forces. Chief knew the attacking force would also be well trained and well armed.

The approaching RHIB was spotted a hundred yards out. Conditions were incredibly bad. The night goggles and their protection from the wind and waves gave *Heaven*'s forces a slight advantage against the invaders from the water. Chief couldn't believe his luck; one boat with maybe six men on this suicide mission, headed straight to hell against *Heaven*'s defenders. It became apparent that Zeta was beyond pissed about this territorial violation by Sinaloa. The plan was obviously to pull off this attack on land, but they were forced to retaliate by sea. Zeta was sacrificing six men out of pure spite.

The RHIB headed toward the port quarter of *Heaven* where they would attempt to board the ladder. As soon as the last man from the RHIB secured his position on the ladder, Chief ordered his men to open fire.

The assault team was completely exposed on the ladder and unable to return effective fire. Ten men with AK-47s ripped bullets across the invaders essentially trapped on the boarding ladder. It was over in fifteen seconds. The next volley of shots from *Heaven* sank the RHIB. By the time the firing stopped, the six attackers were floating away on the angry waves. The only injury to the defending crew was one man, wounded in the thigh by a deflected bullet.

Chief was a trained mercenary. He still felt the slight pang of loss for six good men for no good reason. They died to assuage the ire of brain-dead mobsters. It came as no comfort to Chief that his handlers would do the same, just as easily, if it served their purpose.

While Chief was not a reflective man and he rarely looked fate in the eye, he found he could not control the darkness that gripped his soul at that moment. He had become Satan's angel in that moment. There was no escape. There was no hope. The darkness of his soul was impenetrable.

Captain Corley sipped his dark roast coffee as he pondered his predicament.

"What the hell, Frank? Here we are, honest seamen, just trying to make a living, and we find ourselves in the middle of a drug war. We don't have control over our own crew, even if we considered them 'our' crew. It looks like we survived this fight, but now you and I are legally responsible for the illegal cargo that may be aboard. You and I will be the ones that go to jail if we get caught."

"Captain," said Frank, "I hate to tell you this, but being captured by the authorities might be the lesser of the evils. The Zeta know the name of our ship. They can easily find out our destination. Zeta could turn us in, attack again with more force at sea, or wait until we arrive in port to attack us. We also may be sacrificial goats. Chief can take his men off the boat on some prearranged plan and leave us for arrest or another assault. We know little or nothing, except that we're in possession of drugs. I've heard that the cartels sacrifice the occasional shipment to appease the DEA. We're set up as the goat pretty well."

"Gee," said Corley, "thanks for reminding me that we may be the bull's-eye for a lot of crazy crooks. We have to report this to the home office. Hell, we're at their mercy. Not a place I like to be."

"Too bad we aren't politicians," Frank replied. "They can always blame someone else for their own stupidity. You and I … we got no place to hide."

Corley picked up the encrypted mobile satellite phone to call headquarters in Belize City. When he finally made contact, he reported the event in detail. The supervisor listened without comment, and after several eternal minutes of no exchange, he put the captain on hold. Twenty minutes passed before another voice, a voice Corley did not recognize, broke the silence.

"Captain Corley," the voice said, "we have received an update on the storm, indicating that it is moving northwesterly toward Corpus Christi. You should have an opening southeast, so we are directing you to continue in the Florida Straits on past Key West and make way to Jamaica. We can take on more cargo and reroute you at that time. You are instructed not to report the attempted hijacking to the coast guard."

In a vain attempt to cover his ass, the captain asked the unknown voice, "What is my cargo, and is this crew going to remain on board?"

"Captain, don't waste my time," was the reply. "You have the manifest; the crew is under your command. I should not need to remind you of a captain's duties and responsibilities."

The captain broke contact and returned to the task of navigation.

"Based on my calculations, Frank, we should be in gale-force conditions around midday tomorrow. As we make our turn easterly, we'll be hitting the Gulf Stream, which is always rough. From there we should have smooth sailing to Jamaica. Besides, I'm getting hungry, and that's a sure sign things are improving!"

Nathan was satisfied that the cargo ship could handle the storm unless some problem developed with the rudder or with the engines. With any such malfunctions, they would end up on Campeche Bank in a serious situation.

The reefer cargo ship was a dual prop, approximately 250 feet long by 40 feet in width, tonnage 1416, and could make a speed of thirteen knots. The ship could easily handle the crew of twenty-two and the eleven guards. While the ship was sound, it was terrible seamanship to take on a storm just for the hell of it. The original instructions by headquarters would have them sailing thirty degrees north until they were around the Yucatan Peninsula, north of Cancun, Mexico. From there he would turn easterly toward Key West. Depending on the track of the storm, it would appear at that point that they would be heading directly into the right wall of the hurricane, which was the strongest quadrant. The new instructions, along with the track of the hurricane turning in the direction of Corpus Christi, would make things easier.

Chapter

3

The call from Captain Corley to the home office in Belize was transferred via encrypted telephone and secured mobile devices to the yacht, *Angel*, which was anchored in Lake Izabal. The chief of Sinaloa operations, Salvador Vargas, and "Number One" in Boston, Gilman Loeb, received the call. Real names were never used on the yacht or in Belize. Gilman was known as Sam, and Salvador was known as Max.

The primary reason for their meeting was to supervise the activities of *Heaven* in a critical experiment, testing their ability to ship a product out of Veracruz. The other reason was a restructuring of operations after losing Ken. Changes had to be made. New adaptations were also required for a new banking center in Belize. Policy demanded this kind of critical business be conducted face-to-face.

The storm developing in the gulf had no impact on the weather at Lake Izabal or Fronteras, a frontier town located at the intersection of the only road leading south out of Cancun, Mexico. There was a bridge crossing the lake where Fronteras was located. Fronteras was one of those places where every shop owner kept a shotgun close at hand. The people in town were friendly, but the criminal element was ever present. The price of everything was cheap, the water was beautifully clear, and more than anything, it was easy to hide from prying eyes on Lake Izabal.

The lake also provided a good hurricane hole. It functioned as a yachting safety net when the forces of rain and 80 mph winds made landfall from the gulf impossible. The "hole" was surrounded by strong trees, and the water was deep, but navigation to the shoreline was quick and merciful. If survival meant disembarking, Fronteras accommodated.

The difficulty getting into Lago de Izabal by any large vessel was the bar at the entrance to Amatique Bay, which was only five feet six inches at high tide. Echeneis commissioned Curvelle Yachts to customize *Angel* with a flotation device that would raise the forty-meter craft to a five-feet draft, allowing her to cross the bar. That way, she could avail herself to the benefits of Lake Izabal.

The craft's design was based on a modified racing catamaran hull with two shallow chines. The design had been carefully tested to strike the proper balance for maximum speed, shallow draft, and stability. The draft could be raised with an inflatable device mounted on the hull area between the chines. Unengaged, the inflatable device didn't create a negative drag on the hull speed.

The Bay of Ascension in the Yucatan permitted a protected environment, though not as well as Lake Izabal. Captain Bart Hayes, Ken Renfro's former captain, took *Angel*'s helm after they killed Ken. Hayes likes the security and benefits of both the Bay of Ascension and Lake Izabal. He knew he couldn't actually hide a forty-meter yacht, but he subscribed to the theory that if a tree falls in the forest when there is no human to hear it, then it does not make a sound. If no one was allowed to see the boat, the boat did not exist.

Hayes had an adequate crew designed to keep the bosses happy, and if he needed more help for those special occasions, it was available. The home office in Belize was fully committed to the flagship guest.

While Sam and Max conducted business, Captain Bart smoked his Cuban cigar on the aft deck, counting his lucky stars. It was as if the world were stuck in a prehistoric time, he thought. He looked at the pristine jungle and in his mind envisioned a pterodactyl flying out of the dark mass of trees and swooping up a native fisherman for a morning snack. Bart was adding a few people to the imaginary breakfast menu when he was interrupted by Sam and Max. They, too, were after a smoke.

"Can we join you, Captain?" asked Sam.

"Absolutely, boss," the captain replied.

As Sam and Max lit their cigars, a beautiful native girl slowly rounded the aft of *Angel* in her dugout canoe. Sam choked on his first draw. Bare-breasted, golden skin, with a big smile, she captured their attention as a true gift from the gods. This exquisite creature fixed her eyes on each man, blessing them one by one with a coy wink. Their libidos were pinged into a state of unison bliss.

"Get your brains out of your pants, Max. We got work to do."

Sam had broken the spell.

"Yeah, I hear you talking," was the reply, "as if you're too old to appreciate that gift from heaven. That's the kind of woman that makes the world go around."

"Well, I have to agree with you on that, Max. A girl like that can lead a man to hell and back."

Captain Bart had to turn away to hide his smile. He didn't want them to know she was one of his regulars. She was a gift from god in more ways than these guys could possibly imagine.

Captain Bart didn't envy Sam and Max. He did not know their real names or where they fit into the company that employed them. He could, however, sense their power. It radiated from them like the smell of garlic. People who exercise the power of life and death over others are forever changed in ways he could not express. He had been there. He knew the signs. He had seen it. Sam and Max bore the mark of evil, as did the captain himself. He was confident that these two had given him the order to feed Ken Renfro to the fish. Captain Bart had no regrets, despite the fact that he liked Ken. Such was life.

Captain Bart had to admit to himself that Ken was a much nicer guy than either of these guys. The decision about who lived and who died was not his to make. That job was solely the responsibility of his bosses. His job was to carry out orders. All of their commands might bear the mark of the devil, but Hayes was happy it was not his burden to decide who lived and who died in the operations.

The captain's mother may have taught him that the road to heaven is narrow and there are few who find it, but the road to hell is a well-traveled and often crowded highway. If so, it was a lesson long forgotten.

Having released himself from liability, his cigar began to taste a little better. He sat down in a deck chair, closed his eyes, and reminded himself, *I have a plumb job. I have a great boat over which I am the lord and master. All I have to do is keep this yacht shipshape, keep the crew in line, keep everyone's mouth shut, and keep the bosses happy the few times they actually show up. From time to time, I may be called upon to take lethal action. That's just part of the job. So what?*

Sam and Max finished their cigars and headed back inside to finish their business. They had been at it for several hours. The captain liked that. *Out of sight, out of mind,* he thought. With the bosses back inside, he was alone to ponder his favorite subject, the local native women. Perhaps, at the dawn of time, all women were like these women of Lake Izabal: beautiful, open, and uninhibited about sex. Maybe that was what the gods had intended. Maybe the gods had meant sex to be that way.

The girl in the canoe had an equally beautiful sister, Lola, who worked in his kitchen. Sometimes he would have sex with both of them at the same time. The thought was almost more than Captain Bart could process. These native girls loved to have white babies. The women had developed their own cues and sequences. When one of them would become pregnant, she would step aside, and the next girl in line would step up to take care of the captain's needs.

Captain Bart was not a religious man. As he pondered life, he was surprised when he received an epiphany. Perhaps he was proof that God allows the sun to shine on the good and bad alike. The sun shined on him, so thanks.

Captain Bart leaned back in his deck chair and took another long drag on his cigar. He thought about Sam and Max and couldn't help but smile. He knew they liked each other, contrary to the case with other people in the same filthy business. The norm was that guys like Sam and Max usually ended up killing each other, not making nice-nice. Whatever, Captain Bart didn't care. In fact, he was happy these two idiots played well together in the proverbial sandbox.

Max and Sam could pass as cousins. Sam was a wiry five feet ten and weighed in about 170 pounds. Max was five feet nine and 180 pounds. Their skin was olive; their hair was coal-black. To the average eye, both men could operate in their business without attracting too much attention. Their mannerisms were refined. Although fluent in English, Max sounded foreign in his speech. Sam's accent was more pronounced. Neither man was too flashy or too loud, and both were capable of fitting in any business group, church, or high-society function. These abilities were valuable talents in the high levels of criminal activity. Captain Bart decided that neither man looked like the dangerous crooks they actually were.

After enjoying their cigars and another look at a fine set of tits, the men were refreshed as they retreated to the conference room. At this point, they were alone with their charts and iPads, and Captain Bart was happily alone on the deck.

Sam settled himself into his comfortable chair, sipped his cognac, and looked over at Max. "Now that we have *Heaven* sailing safely to Jamaica, what's your opinion, Max, on our ability to use Veracruz as a transfer point in our drug operation?"

"Sam, I think we proved that our crew can handle the Zeta. Veracruz is big enough to handle both our operations. We didn't attack their operation, and they should be able to live with the fact we are only using Veracruz as a transfer point. In the future, none of us will be able to exclude other gangs from an entire section of Mexico or the U.S. We have to develop a live-and-let-live policy."

"I agree," said Sam. "As you know, we have not had a history of cooperation here in Mexico, but hopefully we can make a little progress on that."

"Not to change the subject, Sam, we still must decide what we are going to do with Captain Corley and Frank Parsons. They know nothing of our real business. Of course they know we bought fish for practically nothing, and now they suspect we're transporting drugs. They will have to become part of the team or be eliminated."

Sam ran his hand through his hair. "On our next shipment, Max, we bring them into our confidence. If they cooperate fully, we will keep them on. If not, your boys can deal with them as usual. In the meantime, have our security keep a close watch on them."

"That's a good plan, Sam." Max followed by letting Sam know that Ken had been replaced by Larry Alexander and Ken Upshaw in directing the Belize banking operations.

"Too bad Ken had to go," remarked Sam. "On the other hand, it looks like Larry and Ron have a greater ability to manage the various tentacles of our foreign operations without unnecessary documentation."

Sam continued his review of the international headquarters that moved to Belize and noted that it would be much easier for the syndicate to profit from the crumbs scraped off the legal operation by the use of their friendly bank. Max concluded that Sam's plan was good. Sam noted that they would continue the US operations and help oversee the Belize operation, and Sam would continue to handle the enforcement operations.

"There is one item of unfinished business, Sam. What are we going to do about Chic Sparks?"

"You mean that choir boy psychologist? Hell, we need to kill his ass."

"Fine. We'll take care of it," snarled Max, his evil eyes flashing.

The remainder of their time was directed toward their primary reason for the joint venture: direction of some of the profits into each of the accounts of principal members in Boston and Mexico. The primary method was to direct funds into bearer bonds, physical possession of gold, diamonds, precious metals, and liquid assets that could be quickly converted to cash. If they could take ownership of a company where the real party in interest could be hidden, they would occasionally make such an investment.

A full accounting on a regular basis was necessary to make certain that each member was allotted the same amount of assets. Once assets were turned over to the member, the responsibility then was theirs alone. No records were kept that would allow any investigation to discover who got what asset. This function was always handled personally by Sam and Max in their face-to-face meetings. Their power in this regard was final. Their word was law.

Once the individual members were given their share, the syndicate provided a secure safe located in a secure room located beneath the bank in Belize. Each man had a secure ten-by-twenty safe within the hardened room. Only the members had access to the hardened room through a hidden access room located in an adjoining building.

Sam's favorite form of relaxation was to lie back in a comfortable chair, smoke a Cuban cigar, and mentally count his gold bars, coins, diamonds, bearer bonds, and liquid goodies secured in his safe. By the time he counted his $50 million, he would have finished his cigar and would be fast asleep. *Beats the hell out of counting sheep*, he thought.

As usual, the men concluded the meeting with a salute to Echeneis as they touched their glasses of Henry IV cognac. Each man boarded his helicopter as it landed on the helipad. Off they would go in separate directions to ports unknown to anyone on *Angel*.

Chapter

4

Salvador Vargas (Max) was meeting with the leaders of the Sinaloa gang to plan their next move in their running battle with the Zeta. He was still pissed at the attack on his freighter, *Heaven*. A response was in order, notwithstanding his men managed to kill the entire attacking force. Sam asked him to drop it. "That's overkill, Max. Overkill always leads to more problems, which have to then be solved."

Max listened to Sam on this point, but he preferred the Mexican way. Zeta had a price to pay for their attack on the ship, and it had to be the Mexican way.

The night air was pleasant as the brain trust of the Sinaloa sat on Salvador's open veranda. The cooks were barbequing one half a steer in the Central American fashion. Salvador took a big draw on his Cuban cigar, slowly exhaled the smoke, looked around to make sure they were safe, and then called the meeting to order.

"Gentlemen, we are here to decide how we are going to punish Zeta for attacking our ship, *Heaven*. This was a direct challenge to our ability to ship our product freely in the Gulf of Mexico. We are still able to operate in the gulf, but I'm tired of these bastards nipping at our heels."

Jose chimed in. "Yeah, boss, we need to chop some heads off. Maybe kill a few family members. That'll get their attention. We've been too passive lately. They might be getting the idea we've turned into a bunch of pussies."

"You know, boss," said Miguel, "Jose might be right. We've gotten so involved with our Boston bankers that we've sort of forgotten that judicious use of violence is necessary, especially here in Mexico. The Boston boys are so afraid of adverse publicity that they have been able to tap us down a little bit. I agree we shouldn't stir up anything publically in the U.S. Our job is to keep Zeta in line and out of our business here in Mexico."

Salvador (Max) leaned back in his chair, propped his feet up on the table, took a sip from his wine glass, took a drag on his big cigar, and as was his fashion, took a pregnant pause as he contorted his face into what looked like the image of deep thought. "Men, I've been thinking. Why don't we go after their head banker in Monterrey? They are totally dependent on this guy to handle all of their money. They are nowhere near as modern and versatile as we are. They don't own their own bank. If we wipe him out, they are in deep trouble. We'll put Josh on the job."

"Boss, what if they go after our bankers?" asked Jose. "Aren't we just as vulnerable as they are?"

"Not by a long shot. We own our own bank in Belize, which is the base of our operations. We actually control the guys who run the bank. If there is ever a fallout, those guys are loyal to us. With our banker's help, we all have accumulated assets in our own individual control all over the world. Our assets are also separated from our banker's assets. And, El Chapo's money is always separated from ours. If they die tomorrow, we would continue with the same business plan, simply in the hands of new bankers. We have people in our employ who have been trained to take the banking responsibility if necessary. We would have to locate a couple of US bankers, but this would only slow us down for a short time. We need to remember that we owe a great deal to Boston for keeping us dedicated to a flexible and profitable business plan. Give me a vote, yes or no."

Jose and Miguel were on board. "Boss," said Miguel, "let me do the job. I need the action."

"Can't do it, Miguel. We can't afford to lose you. We can't afford the action to come back to us. We'll have Josh get one of his friends out of Colombia to handle the job. Zeta will know we did it, but they won't have any proof."

Julius Ferdinand was a powerful banker in Monterey, Mexico, who controlled an extensive empire throughout Central and South America. Josh was well acquainted with Julius. He would develop a plan to take him out in grand style.

Max called Josh on one of his safe phones. "Josh, this is Max. The boys have approved your plan to handle Julius. Are you ready?"

"Yes, Max, I'm on the job as we speak."

"In the way of background, Josh, our people have determined that Julius takes his safety seriously. He always drives in an armored car. He always has four professional bodyguards around him. When he travels, he also has several gang members in the area and at least two additional lookouts. His weakness is his avid support of the arts. He can always be counted on by the symphony orchestra as well as the ballet companies. He has been known to fill in, if needed, as the first violinist in a professional string quartet."

"Max, that's how we'll get him. Julius has arranged for a group of friends to have a private preconcert dinner at his club in Monterey for a special concert being held in his honor. Julius considered this location very safe. He arranged for a full epicurean affair, white gloves and all. It will be far and away the best meal this group of twelve will ever eat.

"Max, I've had my associates plotting every move Julius makes, and everything points to an attack at the club. We're already working on arrangements to carry out the job."

"That's great," said Max. "That's the reason we're giving the job to you. You're the best."

"We actually know, Max, the date and time of the epicurean dinner. This kind of activity will require some extra staff, including at least one extra master chef."

"Okay, Josh, you take care of the details. "

Josh knew that there were several world-class chefs at the Sinaloa's resort in Belize. Josh made one call and set the plan into motion. On the noon flight from Cancun to Monterey was, in Josh's view, the most beautiful chef in the world. She was a five foot eleven beauty from Colombia named Judith. At five o'clock that same afternoon, she was hired as a temporary chef for the special event. Josh would have been shocked if she had not been hired. Among her many talents, Judith spoke French, and her specialty was French cuisine. The head chef was French. He fell in love with Judith at first sight.

This beauty had turned out to be useful to Josh on more than one occasion. The fact that Judith was also a student of the fine art of lovemaking only enhanced her attraction for him. Being a coldblooded killer to boot made her priceless. With her gifts, getting a man into a vulnerable position, unprotected, was child's play. Julius, however, had demonstrated no history of chasing women, so the plan they worked out was designed uniquely for Julius.

Judith and Josh met in a small restaurant on the outskirts of Montercy. "Judith, are you satisfied with the plan?"

"Yes, Josh. Well, I didn't know the head chef was such a lover boy. I've had to satisfy his hunger a couple of times. You don't really care, do you?"

"No, just save some for me. What I was referring to is our plan for Julius."

"Oh, sure. We're in good shape. I have it worked out to switch one of the flower arrangements on Julius's table before the event starts. Fortunately for us, the club has several extra vases they are using for this event. They are large enough to do the job. When will you have the device ready?"

"I'll have it delivered to you the morning of the event before you go to work. At a convenient point during preparations, you can knock one of the arrangements to the floor. That will give you the opportunity to switch the arrangement to the rigged vase. Of course, you could prepare a special arrangement for Julius and make a big deal in a special presentation. If that doesn't work out, you can simply attach the device under the table, but it will be better to use the flower arrangement in the vase."

"How far can I go from the building before I activate the device?"

"As soon as you walk out the back door, you may activate the device. You can go a good distance, but don't. You will need to be sure that Julius is at his seat before you walk out the door. Walk out the door, activate the device, and walk calmly down the driveway. We will be waiting for you."

"Sounds good, Josh. Now finish your steak. You and I need to go party. You know how a little action makes me horny."

"Judith, you're some kind of bad ass. To hell with the steak. Let's get out of here."

"If Julius could just know what kind of unbridled pleasure he will bring to me, he might be able to smile as he departs this life for his great reward in the hereafter."

Hand in hand, like teenage lovers, Josh and Judith walked the two blocks to Josh's hotel. Josh had no problem spending Sinaloa's money. He had the best room in the best hotel in Monterey. Josh had barely shut the door before Judith shed her clothes. What a sight! Judith, always the aggressor, was tearing at Josh's clothes before he could remove his hand from the doorknob, pulling him toward the king-sized bed. For these two, a king-sized bed was necessary to contain their active mating habits.

This was not the first time Judith and Josh had celebrated their mutual sexual desires together. Judith had tested Josh's abilities and had found him uniquely qualified to satisfy her needs. Few men could leave her as exhausted as he could.

Early the next morning, they both lay in bed, satisfied with their night of unfettered debauchery.

"Josh, I only have one regret about this job."

"Yeah? And what would that be?"

"We won't be here long enough for me to abuse your body. So, big boy, you're going to have to take care of me every chance we can make the time. You understand that, don't you?"

"Judith, my body I will gladly give you. After all, you are the best piece of ass in the world."

"If you have the energy, big boy, roll over here and talk nasty into my ear."

"Gladly!"

Judith faced the day of the party with the certainty that all would go well, at least for her. Judith went out of her way to hug and kiss all the help as they came in. Life had favored her in many ways. Today was no exception. The guest arrived in their finest clothes. The waiters were dashing in their tuxes and white gloves, and the chefs were decked out in their tall white hats. The flowers on the table were beautiful, and she was the hit of the party, as always.

After the usual pre-event chatter, all the guests took their seats. Judith observed that Julius placed himself in the middle where he could receive the proper praise for this event from his guests. Judith was sure that most of the guests had never been treated to a real epicurean feast and were truly impressed.

Judith listened carefully as Julius spoke: "Gentlemen, let me welcome you to this event tonight. When we finish here, we will all go across the street and listen to the production of *Carmen*. As the leaders in Monterey, you have earned the position of highest esteem. You are leaders in government, in business, in charities, and in other community activities needed by the common people in Monterey.

"Each of you will find in front of you an iPad Pro, properly engraved with your name in memory and celebration of this event. It is truly my pleasure to be surrounded by an august assembly such as you. Now, let us eat, drink, and make merry."

Judith's interest was to make sure Julius did not change anything that would affect her plan. She saw that nothing had been changed that would affect the timing of the plan.

The guests stood and raised their glasses in salute to Julius. All were aware of his power as the financial genius who controlled billions of dollars of cartel money. Seated here with this very powerful man was almost like being blessed by the pope. Perhaps financially it was better than being blessed by the pope. Unlike the pope, Julius exercised real power.

Judith handled herself in a way to gain attention. She was decked out in a short black-and-white dress with a stylish chef's hat. Her large breasts were pushed up for all to see. If she leaned over just right, the guests were rewarded with a good view of her nipples. It was an exciting view, but most of the men could not pull their eyes from her ass, which was only covered with white string bikini panties. There was very little left for one's imagination. Judith enjoyed the banter with the guests.

Judith directed her attention to Julius, treating him like a baby. With each course, she would personally feed and pamper Julius. "Now, Julius, let me straighten your napkin. Can I get you more water? Would you like extra wine?" Each time afforded her an opportunity to expose her breasts or grab his hand in hers and clinch them to her breasts. She had Julius eating out of her hand. He managed to grab her ass at least a couple of times. He got no resistance. She rewarded him with several views of her ass and managed to rub against him several times. Surely by accident.

Judith was having so much fun with the guest she decided to take the grand exposure of her lovely ass into the kitchen. While the chef and crew were excited to be so entertained, she did manage to slow down the operation. She managed to render what normally was a smooth, classical epicurean affair into a rather drawn-out peep show with excellent food. This crowd of men was totally into the show being put on by Judith; they were not complaining.

Judith managed to hit every table with some display of her assets. Before the main dish was served, Judith got the special flower arrangement she had designed and got the female servers to join her in making a special presentation to Julius. Everything was in place. The beautiful vase containing the explosives sat directly in front of Julius. The lady waitresses joined Julia in singing a version of "For He's a Jolly Good Fellow" and then led the guests into a spontaneous toast to Julius on the special occasion.

Judith was impressed with Julius, who looked like a really nice guy. She enjoyed her chance to entertain him as a parting gift. She saw the smile on his face and gave a return smile as she managed to rub herself against him as she turned to leave the head table. As she was walking toward the side door, breaking off from the other servers who were headed to the kitchen, she concluded that we all have to die, so why not with a smile on your face. She cherished her ability to help start that final journey with all of these gentlemen, smiling a big smile as she passed by. She made it a great point to stop at several tables on the way out and kiss at least one of the guys and whisper in his ear, "Love you!"

Judith stepped outside, turned, and made sure that everyone was in place and engrossed in the main dish, which was being served at the time. Judith was satisfied that she had completed her task with all the aplomb possible. She flipped the switch to on, walked a few paces, and pressed the red button. All hell broke loose. Julius and his important guests all lay dead on the floor. She turned long enough to observe the waiters near the table were likewise killed. As she continued to walk down the driveway toward the waiting car, she noticed that those who were still moving around were running toward the exit, screaming and falling over each other. At that point, no one noticed the beautiful woman casually walking down the driveway to the street, where she entered a waiting vehicle. Judith was taken directly to the airport, allowing just enough time to change clothes. When she exited the car in the sunglasses, wig, and dowdy dress that came a little below her knees, she looked totally different. She boarded the flight to Cuba. From Cuba, she would take a puddle hopper to Belize City.

Other than a fleeting memory of the beautiful young chef, there would be no record of her real identity. Her passport, name, and all official documents she used were forged. The survivors began to question whether this beauty was real or simply an apparition produced by the trauma of the explosion.

Chapter

Chic's fears that he was going to be called back into the case involving Ken Renfro came to life when he received a voicemail from Dr. Fletcher Renfro asking that he call him. Chic returned Dr. Renfro's call and arranged a meeting at Dr. Renfro's home. Chic arranged the meeting for a Saturday afternoon when Vanderbilt didn't have a football game scheduled. Chic had checked and knew that Dr. Renfro was a Vanderbilt football fan.

Dr. Renfro met with his family prior to Chic's arrival. The whole crowd was there: Ann, Ken's mother, and a retired nurse, Dr. Myra North, Ken's sister, a professor of English at Vanderbilt University, and Dr. John Renfro, his brother who was a neurosurgeon. Dr. Renfro's house was very nice and in a great neighborhood, but it couldn't be classified as a mansion. Dr. Renfro had done well in his family practice. This family group was certainly financially capable of underwriting at least a basic investigation into the present whereabouts of Ken.

As was the practice with Chic, he pulled up to the front door at 2:00 p.m. and rang the doorbell a little ahead of schedule. Ann, Dr. Renfro's wife, opened the door. "Mr. Sparks, I assume."

"Yes, ma'am, and with me is Suzy." Suzy was a petite, redheaded bombshell, outgoing and captivating. She taught gym in college, and her physical fitness was obvious. Until she encountered Chic, she had been a fully committed rounder. Together, Chic and Suzy made everyone's list of first among the pretty people.

"Come on in and let me introduce you to the family."

After the introduction, Chic took over.

"Folks, it is a real pleasure to meet with you today. I want you to know that Ken was my friend. I can't tell you what all he was into, but he left me this handwritten note at his house." Chic gave Ann a copy of Ken's note. "In fact, this note is the only thing we found in the house. In spite of our diverse views about the meaning of life, I called Ken my friend.

"I can tell you that regardless of what you and your family decide about my cost, I'm going to continue to do what I can to find Ken. I would like to be optimistic about finding him alive, but I fear the worst. To this point, I have used all of my police resources to find him but to no avail. I have not been able to locate his boat, *Amedee*. I have not been able to locate a single asset of his that was not foreclosed on."

"Chic," said Ann, "Myra and John also believe he might be dead. They say that a person with his assets, more than $20 million or so, doesn't just disappear into thin air along with all the assets. Is that true?"

"First, I think that Ken had substantially more than $20 million," said Chic. Then he addressed the entire group. "Folks, I hoped that you could give me some tidbit of information that might turn out to be beneficial. For example, I hoped Ken had sent you a postcard or made some effort to contact you on birthdays and Christmas but obviously not. Apparently, none of us actually has any solid information about his boss or the name of someone he actually worked with. Is that true?"

All agreed that this was true.

"I'm actually embarrassed that I never cared enough to press Ken for his personal information. I'm amazed that I failed to observe any warning signs that Ken was living a double life. I have to admit that this failure causes me to question whether I really was concerned about my friend's soul and his general well-being. Hopefully this is a life lesson learned about how we actually show our interests in the well-being of others. Thank you for allowing me the chance to fret over my shortcomings.

"Now, I'm here for two reasons. One is, after talking to Dr. Renfro, he expressed some interest in helping with the expenses of my investigation.

In view of the time it will take from my practice and the fact that I will get no financial help from the sheriff's office, I actually need a little financial help. Secondly, sooner or later, the most likely source of information about Ken is you. So you need to probe your letters and cards and dig into any information you got from Ken in the last four or five years—or any clues about his business contacts. Be sure to get that information to me.

"I understand that Ann is going to take me into the back room and beat me around a little bit until I agree with her terms. Ann, are you ready?"

"Follow me to the kitchen, Chic. We'll leave Suzy in here to entertain the children. Oh, I forgot about Fletcher. I think she can handle him as well."

"Don't worry about her, Ann. Suzy can handle her own."

By now, Chic had developed some rapport with this family. They were good people. Chic couldn't cast blame on Ken's family for his sins. Ken's sins were his own. Chic was convinced that if he was fortunate enough to have three children, he could only hope that two of them would be as exemplary as Myra and John.

Chic actually enjoyed head banging with Ann. It was a lot like dealing with his mother. After about thirty minutes, they came to a reasonable deal. Chic was not going to be made whole, but he would be getting enough financial assistance to make the effort feasible. The next thirty minutes they spent cracking jokes, and Chic, of course, took most of the time fishing family history out of Ann.

They completed their business, and Chic followed Ann to look at Ken's old bedroom, which yielded no useful information.

Suzy entertained the rest of the family while waiting for Ann and Chic to return. The great thing about Suzy was her positive, upbeat attitude and her lack of inhibition. It was hard to be a stranger around Suzy. By the time Chic and Suzy bid the Renfros adieu, the two of them had developed an affinity toward the Renfro family. Once again, Suzy impressed Chic with her intelligence and her gift of reading people. The group gathered back together and said their good-byes, and Chic and Suzy left.

"Well, Chic, did you learn anything helpful?"

"I learned a lot about Ken's family, I think, but nothing really helpful to the investigation. They certainly give the appearance of an exemplary family—highly educated and positive community leaders. I'd have to say that on my first impression, I'm in awe of the family. I believe that if Ken were alive, he would have contacted them. He may be the black sheep of the family, but he did stay in contact, at least on special occasions. I detected some evidence that Ken liked to brag about his wealth to his folks, just to prove he had achieved more than the whole crowd of them combined.

"I also think the family was a little irritated that Ken was able to disappear along with his wealth. I think they need to believe that Ken is dead. If he's not dead, they would have to accept that Ken deceived them and devised a plan to deny them any of his wealth. From my point of view, Suzy, it took careful planning to place mortgages on all his assets and have them held by legitimate companies that were prepared to foreclose as quickly as legally possible after he disappeared. Only the FBI or IRS could pierce this veil and determine whether the loans were real or bogus. In fact, this method could be used to advance money to Ken when he got to his destination. The loan to value was low, so the mortgage company would not have lost money.

"The key part is that if Ken was disposed of, this method would have placed all Ken's assets into the hands of the criminal enterprise, eliminating any battle over assets by his estate. Without this method, the criminal enterprise would be in court trying to protect Ken's assets, which they would consider their assets. The criminal enterprise would need to avoid this outcome at all costs."

Chic fell silent for a long time. He concentrated on the road. A red pickup truck cut him off, and Chic had to slam on brakes to avoid a collision. Suzy squealed and shot her arms out to brace herself.

"Thank God you've got good reflexes, Chic!"

Emergency avoided, Suzy fixed her hair and sat up straight. "Let's see if you can get us to Anniston, Chic, where my mom and my family are waiting on us. I know you can't wait."

"Sweetie pie, you know I'll follow you anywhere, even to Sand Mountain, Alabama." Chic had the feeling that by the time he met all the Sand Mountain folks, his definition of "anywhere" might well be exponentially enlarged.

Chapter

6

The next morning, Chic and Suzy were in the parking lot of Waffle House, located next to Quintard Mall in Anniston, Alabama. They had a five-minute wait until Suzy's mother, Margie, showed up with Suzy's uncle Dean. Margie came right up to Chic, gave him a bear hug, and kissed him on the cheek.

Chic was a big guy, six foot three, 215 pounds, with blond, wavy hair, and had the general appearance of a Nordic god. He projected strength beneath this veneer. He graduated from Florida State with an AB in criminal justice. He was known from college as a world-class tenor and had gotten better with age. He completed ranger training at Fort Benning, Georgia, and saw service at several hot spots in the world. In civilian life, he completed his doctor's degree at Florida State in clinical psychology.

"Wait a minute. I'm not bashful. Margie, I can see where Suzy gets her red hair and zest for life. It's a real pleasure to meet you." Chic returned the hug along with a kiss.

Margie, at five foot five, was a little smaller than Suzy, who was five seven and 110 pounds. Although Margie was a good-looking woman, Suzy, at thirty-five and in her prime, did not take a backseat to anyone in that department. Her red hair was a little darker than Suzy's. Margie's accent was more pronounced and bore the mountain twang, which Suzy had lost. Otherwise, these two couldn't deny their mother-daughter relationship. *God was in a good mood the day he breathed life into these two*, thought Chic.

"Momma, I hope you don't mind our dropping in like this. We were in Nashville, and I decided it was time you met the love of my life, Chic.

I knew you would like to meet him since he's a looker and a music man. Momma, he's not a country singer. Chic here's a real opera star."

"Lord, Suzy, I've never met a real opera singer! You'll have to excuse my daughter, Chic. I'm not really that kind of gal. Well, I will confess that you are a looker, but mainly I'm impressed that she has found a real man. You know what they say: a good man is hard to find."

Chic actually did flash a little blush at that. He had no doubt that Margie had the same fire in her soul as did Suzy. "Okay, ladies, quit giving me the big head. Suzy knows how easy it is to pull my chain. What have you got planned for us today, Margie?"

"I thought we'd have breakfast here at the Waffle House and then maybe go to the Sacred Harp singing. You know I like to go with your uncle Gus to the yearly music camp. Since Chic is a music man, I thought he might enjoy the experience. Now, Chic, are you sure you like this old-timey music?"

"You know, Margie, I had no idea that people still sing shape note music or follow the Sacred Harp routine. I would be delighted to see and hear this living history firsthand. The last time I heard Sacred Harp was on an early Sunday morning TV show. I think that group came out of Defuniak Springs, Florida, but I'm not certain of that. Rather than the technique itself, I'm fascinated with the musical meter and unique sound, which I have used in choir work. When the choir sings some of the old traditional hymns, it's good to imitate, in a loose way, the sound of a Sacred Harp choir. Where is the camp?"

"We have Sacred Harp singing up here in Sand Mountain every year. This year we're going to Camp McDougle between Double Springs and Jasper."

Chic quickly adapted to the Sacred Harp method of arranging the choir in a square, with the director in the middle surrounded by the tenors, bass, altos, and sopranos. The group couldn't believe their good fortune when Chic sang several of his favorite songs, including, "Flee as a Bird to Your Mountain" by Dana Shindler, 1842.

The four of them stayed until late afternoon when the attendees enjoyed a good meal under the trees. In a strange way, this place and these people reminded Chic of his favorite place on earth: Vortex Springs, near Ponce De

Leon, Florida. To Chic, Vortex Springs was the essence of redneck-ism. It harkened back to rural America's honest, hardworking Christian farmers ... a time that no longer existed. That spirit still resounded in Chic's soul as well as with the camp-singing devotees. Only at Vortex Springs could you see people parked in pickup trucks surrounding the spring, cooking barbeque, scuba diving in the cold deep spring, and kids swinging into the spring from steel cables suspended from trees. On every side, there were softball games, volley ball, and horseshoes. Moving in the parade, the mothers in their bright-colored bikinis directed their children to jump in the sixty-five-degree water. The men would sit back in their lawn recliners, throwing their empty beer cans into the beds of their pickup trucks while tending to their cooking duties. Ordained as if part of the ritual, a fight would periodically break out over some sexy lady. What a place!

They finally said their good-byes and got into Chic's car for the trip back to Anniston.

"Okay, Chic," said Margie, "what do you think about the Sacred Harp camp?"

"Quite frankly, Margie, I'm actually surprised that something I thought was basically dead is so alive. I'm not sure that anything in music actually dies. It certainly changes. It adapts to the concerns of the day. So music remains relevant to the emotional needs of the people, as do art and literature. It has always been my belief that the form taken by music, art, and literature is time sensitive. So I really appreciate this learning experience to live and breathe a piece of history."

"You are very welcome," said Margie. "I don't want to give you a big head, but you can come sing to me anytime you want. I think you know these people will never forget that you came, you participated, and you blessed them with your God-given gift. It is the spirit you shared with your wonderful voice that they will never forget."

"Thanks, Margie. I do in fact believe that when you sing, it has to be a joyful gift to God. I have to tell you that the pleasure of this day was all mine."

Gus hadn't managed to get in much talk time with the group. He finally saw an opportunity to speak. "Suzy, you remember your cousin Buck, don't you?"

"Sure I do, but I haven't seen him in several years. I hope he has learned to keep himself out of jail. Every time I hear about him, he's in jail. Either in jail or getting out of jail."

"I saw him the other day, and he asked about you," said Gus. "I think he heard you were in trouble or that somebody was out to hurt you. I know he's always in trouble, but he's in touch with all the crooks up here in the Sand Mountain area. The crooks up here are close to the crooks in the Panhandle of Florida. I think they all like to get drunk and fight chickens together. I believe he wants to see if he can help you in any way."

Suzy crinkled her nose. "I don't know, Gus. Sounds like trouble to me. He's the black sheep of the family."

"Gus," said Chic, "is he expecting Suzy to call him or meet with him tonight?"

"Buck lives on the way back to Anniston. He asked me to call him on the way back if we would."

"Suzy," said Chic, "I think we need to meet with Buck. Crooks do in fact tend to know each other, particularly the ones that fight dogs or chickens. They tend to get the attitude that the world is picking on them, which creates a sort of bond between them."

As they drove to the café, Chic thought back on how close Suzy had come to getting killed during a home invasion. She'd wasted that guy. She'd also managed to escape when her two partners in the threesome were killed by the assassins. It turned out they were now out for revenge. At least that was how it looked.

"Suzy, we need to talk to him. We have nothing to lose by giving him a chance. I only need one lead to find this gang."

"Okay, Chic. Let's do it. Gus, call Buck. See where he wants to meet."

Gus got Buck on the phone and arranged to meet at a little barbeque place in Lincoln, Alabama. They were close to Pell city, within fifteen to twenty minutes of the roadside café in Lincoln. When they got there, Buck was leaning against his old Ford 150, waiting on them. Buck looked the part: pear-shaped body, five feet ten, 255 pounds, looking like a friendly grizzly bear. Dressed in his blue jeans and a black Harley-Davidson shirt, he was not the kind of guy Chic would try to piss off. Chic pegged Buck Chapman as a dangerous man. Even as your friend, you'd have to watch your back. The kind of guy who tells you what a great friend you are while stabbing you in the back. Sort of like a bad dog who doesn't bark before biting.

Buck gave Suzy a big hug and exhibited true affection. To the others, it was a simple grunt.

"Buck, I want you to meet Chic. It's because of him that I'm alive."

"A real pleasure to make your acquaintance, Chic. Put it here." Buck extended his right hand to Chic and grabbed his shoulder with his left hand at the same time.

"Likewise," said Chic. Chic concluded that Buck may look fat, but when he moved, nothing bounced. His grip was solid. Chic concluded that if he had to go somewhere dangerous, Buck would be a good guy to cover his back.

The group went into the rundown café and got drinks and some lemon icebox pie, which was reported to be damn good. Chic was impressed with the pie and concluded that you can't judge a cafe by its cover.

"Tell me what's going on, Suzy. From the papers, all I can tell is some guys tried to kill you because you know something about a robbery, but that's about the extent of it. I know a lot of people in the Panhandle, and I might know somebody that has some useful information. I have a chicken-fighting friend who claims to know somebody that worked on a boat for a really rich guy in Pensacola that just up and disappeared. I thought you might be interested in talking to my friend and see if he knows something that's connected to your situation."

Chic couldn't believe his good luck. "Buck, I can tell you that we've had no good leads in this case, and any chance to talk to your friend would be wonderful. There's only one case of a rich guy disappearing in Pensacola I know of, and that's Ken Renfro, whose family we just visited in Nashville. Can you arrange a meeting?"

"The problem is, Chic, you look too much like a police officer, and I've heard you work with the police. You know even crooks have a code of ethics. They don't help police officers. Chicken fighters, even though most of them think of themselves as perfectly normal, don't like the authorities. Hell, all the authorities ever do is arrest them and confiscate and kill their valuable chickens. Hell, they're dead either way. Besides, a chicken ain't no animal."

"Now that's a fine howdy-do," Buck continued with a snarl. "They go to a chicken fight, which they love to do, and the police come in, confiscate the chickens, and promptly kill them. Then they charge them with cruelty to animals because they let them fight to the death. Now they call that inhumane treatment or cruelty to animals."

Chic smiled. "Well, I must say, Buck, I never really thought about it that way. But it does sound a little shitty, doesn't it?" Chic, of course, was using his best redneck impersonation in his repartee with Buck.

"Buck, I always heard that President Lincoln was a devotee of chicken fighting. I understand that Lincoln felt like chickens should have the same right to kill each other as people. Is that true?"

Buck's face brightened at being given the chance to show he was a pretty smart guy. "You bet your ass that's true, Chic. Excuse my cussing, Suzy. You know sometimes I get a little excited."

"That's just fine, cuz. You're not around any angels here. I've got as much Sand Mountain in me as you do. Before the night is over, you may hear me come out with a cuss word or two."

"Chic, I don't know if my friend is going to talk to you or not. He might talk to Suzy. Then you've got to convince him to introduce you to his friend who actually worked for this rich guy. You see my problem?"

"How do you suggest we handle this, Buck? You'll have to lead the way on this one."

Chic knew that people there normally would not open up to a guy like him. He had managed to get along with Buck fairly well, which was not easy. Chick knew that Buck always seemed to be in a pissing contest with other men. "Mine is bigger than yours." Chic could tell the people there actually feared Buck. Chic knew he had passed the test when he was invited to the chicken fight.

"Have you ever been to a chicken fight, Chic?"

"Never have, but I think you're going to take me to one, right?"

"You bet your ass I am," said Buck. "We've got one in Shreveport next weekend. You and I will be there, and we'll see if you can handle my friends."

"Buck, I've heard a lot of bad things about you chicken fighting guys, but I've managed to survive a lot of close calls. I've been shot at by several guys with evil intent in their red eyes, so I believe I can handle the chicken fight crowd. Besides, Buck, I'll be there with you, and I'm sure you'll help me out if things get too hairy."

"Don't bet your ass on that, Chic. Hell, I might just want to see what kind of shit you've really got. After all, you're just a pussy singer, aren't you?"

"Now listen, Buck, I know you can be a badass, but I don't want to prove my manhood at a chicken fight just so you can have some fun. All I'm trying to do is run down the people who're trying to kill Suzy. To do that, I need your help with your friends. If you can play this straight, then after that you can test my manhood anytime. Just name it."

"Fair enough, Chic. For Suzy, we'll act like big boys at the chicken fight. That's all I can promise."

Chapter

Chic and Suzy met Buck at the Holiday Inn West in Shreveport, Louisiana, just off Interstate 20. Buck had explained that the chicken fight location was in the woods northeast of Shreveport.

Buck, looking very authoritative, explained to Chic, "This particular chicken fight location is not your normal place. It's in the woods but not far off the road. Normally, us chicken fighters like to be out in isolated places away from prying eyes. This one is easy to see because we are told it is the only legal chicken-fighting arena in the U.S. I can't swear on that, but I can tell you we've never been raided here, so you should be safe."

Suzy, giving her best impression of bravery, spoke up. "Now, boys, I'm a pretty game gal, but I don't think I need to go to the chicken fight. I'll hang around the motel, and if you need me, call. I'll come a running."

"We don't normally allow women at the chicken fights, Suzy. It's a man thing. You wouldn't have to worry about the chickens, but there would be a bunch of dirty old men, and Chic and I wouldn't be able to beat the hell out of them all. You stay here and enjoy yourself. This is a job for me and Chic."

"Tell me, Buck, what do you bad boys do at a chicken fight other than watch chickens kill each other, drink whiskey, fight, and gamble?"

"Hell, Suzy, that sounds like enough good reasons to go to a chicken fight for me. Now you did leave out talking dirty about women."

"I guess then you boys would pass the 5F Club that describes a typical redneck weekend: fighting, fishing, frigging, and fixing flats on a Friday night."

"You've got us pegged pretty good there, Suzy. What you don't really know is that a lot of the guys make their living by raising fighting cocks. In fact, that's how I make most of my living. I'm not fighting my cocks today because I couldn't do that and nursemaid you two."

"Okay, Buck," said Chic, "how do you make a living selling fighting cocks?"

"Well, if you notice when you travel, chicken fighting is big in the Caribbean, the Philippines, and a lot of places in South America. People from all over the world fly to America to buy our fighting cocks. We produce the best cocks in the world. If you can get a good reputation, you can sell your fighting cocks for around $1200 each. It's not illegal to sell your chickens. In fact, I had a good friend who was known as the master, who normally got that much for his chickens. His son was a top quarterback at Troy and graduated with honors. He's never had a job. All he does is raise chickens and lives high on the hog doing it.

"Time to go," said Buck.

Chic and Buck got into Buck's Ford 150 pickup truck and headed to the chicken fight. Chic was puzzled at the information that there was a profit behind chicken fighting. He knew they gambled but didn't realize there was a profit to be made simply raising and selling chickens. Maybe he was selling these guys a little short. He should have known that Buck was not the kind of guy who went to cockfights for pure joy. Other than fighting, he didn't read Buck as the kind of guy who did anything for pure pleasure. Buck needed an ulterior motive.

When they arrived at the arena, Chic was identified as a new guy who had never been to a cockfight. The crowd knew Buck well enough that they were confident he would not bring a policeman or an undercover agent to one of his cockfights.

As the fight began, Chic was immediately sucked into the excitement along with the other spectators. Chic promised himself he was going to remain aloof to the frenzy that engulfs sporting events of this nature, but before he knew it, he was indistinguishable from the rest of the wide-eyed, excited, noisy gamblers.

Chic couldn't help but remember his first Mardi Gras in New Orleans. There he was in his tux at a black-tie event for clinical psychologists, calmly watching the parade go by. Dispassionately, he observed the young kids pushing and shoving to get to the doubloons, beads, and other trinkets. *How silly*, he thought. In the next moment, Chic found himself on his knees in the street, elbowing the kids, fighting for doubloons. It took a few seconds before reality set in. From that day to this, he couldn't recall how he actually made the transition from calmly watching little kids fighting for doubloons to becoming like a street urchin.

Maybe the ambient craziness of the Cajun mentality just engulfed me when I went to Louisiana. Well, any excuse is better than none at all.

Chic decided to quit fighting his dark angels and simply go with the flow. It didn't take long to realize that cock fighters were evangelists at heart. Everybody there had a tale to tell the newcomer, which seemed to be directed toward their special gripe about the do-gooders who confiscated their cocks and promptly killed them.

He heard the story about President Lincoln at least a half-dozen times. The paranoia was virtually palpable. The world definitely was not treating these individuals with any respect, at least in their own little world.

As the chicken fight developed, the spectators reached a peak crescendo in harmony with the dominant cock, which spiked and ripped the life out of his opponent. Chic had the distinct feeling that the crowd as one soul engulfed itself in a sexual climax.

After the dominant cock strutted his stuff over the body of the lesser chicken, the crowd settled down long enough to get themselves recharged for the next fight.

Chic observed that this was a group of verbal extroverts passionately involved in a blood sport, the blood of the foul, armed to the teeth and possessed with a monumental nasty attitude. He realized that at the climax, he was in the midst of a throng of what he could only describe as demons.

Chic kept a close eye on Buck and made certain they were in position to see each other at all times. It was obvious that Buck was well known among this group. He knew the ins and outs of the cockfighting scene. Chic made a mental note that while there was a lot of loud talking, shoving, and nose-to-nose confrontation, he didn't see anyone challenge Buck.

As the last fight was beginning, Chic decided it was time to see whether or not Buck was going to introduce him to his friend. At about the same time, Buck motioned to Chic to come over. Chic complied. Buck led Chic to a small table in an out-of-the-way corner, which was used mainly for sharing a few drinks with a buddy. Seated at the table was a square-looking guy who weighed about one half of Buck's weight. He had thick glasses and was generally dressed like a farmer. His black hair looked like some of his chickens had roosted there for several days.

Buck walked over to the table, sat down, and motioned for Chic to sit down.

"Jack, I'd like you to meet my friend here, Chic Sparks. This is the guy who saved Suzy from those guys who tried to kill her over in Pensacola.

"Chic, this here is Jack Quintard, a friend of mine. He lives in Sand Mountain and is one of our best cock fighters."

Chic took his hand and shook it. "Nice to meet you, Jack."

Jack grunted, "Likewise."

"Jack, I told Chic that you knew a guy with a big sailboat over in Pensacola, or at least knew some of the guys who crewed on the boat. Chic is trying to find a guy named Ken who owned the sailboat like you described to me. Chic saved Suzy, and Ken's family has asked Chic to find him. They haven't heard from Ken or seen his sailboat since he disappeared."

"Now, look here," said Jack, "I'm not interested in helping the police. You know how we feel about that, Buck. If I help the police, they won't let me back in Sand Mountain."

"Jack, I understand what you mean," injected Chic. "My purpose here is to help Ken's family and Suzy. Ken was a close friend of mine, and I'd like to make sure he's safe myself. I'm not a police officer. I'm not here to represent the police. I'm a clinical psychologist, and my office is in Pensacola. You can look it up in the phone book. The family asked me to do this for them. Because of my involvement with Ken, they know I'm the only person with enough personal knowledge to maybe find Ken. Then Suzy needs this information for her own safety."

Jack stared for a while at his bourbon and Coke sitting on the table. He took a sip and finally issued a grunt signifying he had reached a decision. He looked up at Chic and issued his decision. "Buck, I actually don't know enough to bother anybody, certainly not enough to help the police. You know if I can help Suzy and not get myself in trouble, I will. Chic, I guess you know this bunch Ken's dealing with will kill you in a second."

"Yes, and I appreciate any help you can give me. Actually, at this point, I don't know enough about what Ken is involved in to know what they're capable of. I'm hoping that all I've got to do here is get enough information on Ken to make his family happy."

"It's like this, Chic. My friend Doug was a cook on the boat named the *Amedee*. I'm not real sure, but I think the guy he worked for was named Ken. That's really all I know about this."

"Jack, how do you know Doug?" asked Chic.

"Doug Barnett is his name. We went to school together in Anniston. His daddy left this area, and I don't know where he is. His mother is dead. If he had any kin folks, I don't know who they are. You know, Buck, old Doug likes to bet on the chickens, so he's been to a few fights with me, but I don't think you know him.

"Doug told me he was the cook on the *Amedee*. He called me from Miami about six months ago about getting him to a cockfight, but he wasn't in Miami long enough for me to set it up."

"Jack, what's the latest you've heard from Doug? Where is he and what's he up to?"

"Well, Chic, he did tell me he's working in Belize now and was a cook on *Angel*, a yacht kept in Belize on some lake south of Belize. I got the impression he was working for the same company as before. He told me he really liked his job on this yacht. Plus he really didn't have much to do. He didn't tell me who he worked for. Old Doug never has been a talker. He did say that Captain Hayes, who was also the captain of the *Amedee*, is the captain of this yacht, *Angel*, which he is now on."

"Tell me, Jack, do you have any way to find Doug?"

"No," said Jack. "Doug made it clear to me it was in my best interest not to try to find him. Mr. Chic, if I were you, I'd take that warning seriously. If you get too close, they may cut your nose off, if you know what I mean."

Chic held Jack in conversation as long as he could but was unable to drag any more information out of him. He realized he would have to find Doug on his own.

Chic looked around at the crowd and concluded that the cast of characters seemed to have been provided by central casting. Chic became acutely aware that he didn't fit the mold. He simply looked like a corporate person or a cop. He could see in the eyes of the crowd that without Buck, he would have to fight his way to his car. He could pick out two or three guys he knew were geared up for combat. All they needed was an excuse.

Chic finally realized that the number-one guy in the house to start a fight was at the table with him—Buck. No one was going to challenge Buck.

It was after midnight when Chic and Buck left the cockfighting arena and headed back to the motel. Both men were happy with the night and managed to do a little singing on the way back. Buck was surprised that Chic knew some of the old mountain tunes.

Chic was totally amazed that he had discovered evidence that would lead him to a specific place where he could interview people who actually knew what happened to Ken. Not only that, he had a shot of discovering the home of the octopus. Chic had no doubt that whoever those people were, they were capable of killing him and everyone he knew without hesitation. He knew he was now a dog with a scent. The call to the hunt wouldn't be drowned out by fear of battle.

Chic couldn't help but recall that time as a seven-year-old that a thirteen-year-old told him he was going to hit him in the nose. Chic took the challenge, stuck his nose toward this big boy, and said, "You and what army?" The big boy struck Chic in the nose as promised, sending him flying down the stairs and into the front yard. Chic, lying on the ground, decided the next time he challenged the big guy, he would put distance between himself and the attacker. Chic realized what he had learned from this event, that he would always accept a challenge, but he also learned that being careful was the better part of valor.

Chic decided that with the problems at hand, stealth was required. A brave frontal attack wouldn't work. Flying down to Belize and trying to find Doug or the boat *Angel* could become a fool's errand. If he directly approached Doug, his life would immediately be in danger. He had to find a less direct way.

Chapter

8

On the way back to Pensacola, Chic gave Suzy a full report on his experience at the cockfight. Chic let Suzy know that he was fascinated with her cousin, Buck. They both agreed that Buck was your worst enemy if he didn't like you and that he didn't like many people. On the other hand, if he decided he liked you, it was an unconditional kind of commitment.

"You know, Suzy, one day I hope to be able to return the favor to Buck. With his help, we obtained information that can lead us forward in this case. It goes to show that you never really can predict where you may get a break in a case."

"Chic, I'm not sure how you plan on using this information. You know that the captain of the *Amedee* is now on a yacht in Belize and that he has a cook named Doug. You know that these two guys knew Ken and worked for him for a number of years. They know his whereabouts. You know these are dangerous men, so you can't just walk up and start asking questions. So, now what?"

"You know how to hurt a guy, don't you? I have absolutely no idea how to get information out of these guys. My basic idea is I will have to go down to Lake Izabal, case the place for maybe a week, and then scope out Belize for a week or so. I should be able to find and identify the yacht *Angel* and maybe identify the captain and Doug. Then I will apply a very scientific method that is left out of all the 101 detective courses. This is called 'allowing the scene to speak to you.'"

"Chic, I probably would say you're full of crap, but I actually believe you. You do seem to have a talent for counterintuitive thinking. More importantly, you actually believe your hunches enough to follow them. So, you're working on a vacation in Belize. What about me?"

"Suzy, I would really like to take you, but this is going to be dangerous. Fronteras is a scenic place but not safe for a beautiful redheaded knockout like you. You would not make a good undercover agent. Before I go, I will work out a plan with Heath to make sure we don't stir up a hornets' nest. If they find out I'm still on their tail, we could be in serious trouble."

Suzy didn't reply for a while. Her eyes were staring out into the distance as the horror of her near-death experience floated into her conscious mind. She felt the presence of evil engulf her. The vision of white-hot breath of an evil spirit left her empty. Her reservoir of strength that had pulled her through her close encounters with death was empty. She began to whimper, and it reached a crescendo as a heart-wrenching wail. She couldn't bear an uncertain future where she would again face evil men who might try to kill her at any moment.

Chic found a place to pull over, where he could devote his full attention to Suzy. In this moment of truth, Chic realized that he was in fact a warrior at heart. The risk, the negative consequences inherent in confronting evil eye-to-eye, the possibility of death to loved ones—none of those life-ending choices worked their power to diminish Chic's commitment to combat.

Suzy discovered the hard way that she was a fighter, but the reality of the consequences of the battle fell upon her like a lead balloon. She knew this was not the time for Chic to practice his psychological bull crap on her. Only his gentle hand and silence would calm her soul. Suzy had to decide whether to join the fight against evil or retire to her corner.

She closed her eyes, practiced deep breathing, and drifted into a state of limbo. As her mind drifted, seeking a safe harbor to hide from reality, a man came from under her bed with knife drawn. Her head hit his as he came up, causing him to pause just long enough for her to reach under her pillow and grab her pistol. She was able to fire the pistol before he could bring his knife to bear. She rolled off the bed and advanced around it, firing once again. The assassin lay dead on the floor. No horror movie could possibly portray the full impact of this event on her psyche. These feedbacks were as real as the true event. She awoke with a scream.

It took awhile, but Suzy finally got herself under control enough for Chic to get back on the road. She huddled as close to Chic as she could. She found strength next to him. It was as though his spirit joined hers, adding the power she lacked. Once again, Suzy realized that facing her mortality for real was not easy. It frightened the hell out of her.

"Chic, I'm sorry I had a meltdown back there. In my mind, I hoped we were out of danger and that we really had no reason to pursue this bunch of crooks. Some part of me wants to retreat to the role of a little, unknown college gym instructor where the problems of the world are not my concern. This mission is not as clear to me as it is to you. I haven't decided to be superwoman yet, and if I do, I don't know how to really help you in this fight. It's a view of my future I can't comprehend."

Suzy recognized that crime fighting chose Chic. He didn't choose this path; it chose him. Their spirits joined together, knowing they were somehow compelled to make their lives together a battle with evil.

"Chic, it makes me feel more connected with the universal and eternal struggle between good and evil to know the battle is bigger than either of us. The evil we're fighting in this case has to be fought by us both. This group out of Boston is deadly. They have proven they are capable of extreme violence against anyone who is a danger to their organization.

"Let me relieve your mind. I'm sorry I panicked when it dawned on me that we continue to be targets. I didn't volunteer for this fight, but I'm here until the end. After you calmed me down, I began to think about some of our Bible lessons on fear. I'm concerned that fear of humankind is totally inconsistent with the teaching of Christ. We are to fear no human, only God, who has power over the body and soul. Christ tells us to fear not, that His yoke is easy. So, Chic, I've decided to live my life without fear of what the boogeyman may do to me. What is that you always say? 'Don't die before you're dead'? I've come to believe that fear of death is exactly that."

"Babe, you are always a source of inspiration to me. We may not solve the problems of the world, but we are going to put this one evil enterprise out of business."

"Does that mean I may play Wonder Woman, Chic?

"You bet, babe. We'll start with the safe stuff. Don't you have a good friend who teaches in the business school who retired as an officer in a large commercial mortgage company?"

"Yes, her name is Nancy Warditch."

"What I plan on doing is getting all my notes I've accumulated on this enterprise and see if you two can establish any patterns that might lead to the parent company. I'm confident you two can come up with some connection among the various companies. We have to have that in order to crack this case."

"I'll talk to her, Chic. I'm sure she'll help. It'll be a pleasure to use my brain again for something other than avoiding killers. I'm afraid gym doesn't challenge the brain."

Chic was satisfied that Suzy had been fighting this battle for a while. Being around home, her mother and kinfolks brought into focus the real danger everyone was in as a result of her involvement with Chic and these drug dealers. Her decision to engage instead of retreating was a deliberate decision, knowing the risk. Suzy was smart as hell. He was happy to have her aboard so they could cover each other's back.

———•———

Chic's premonition was well founded. Before Sam and Max left Belize, they made a decision on Chic and Suzy.

"Alex, Chic and Suzy have cost us the services of Ken Renfro and a lot of resources, setting up our new people in Pensacola and staying clear of his attempted investigation. It's embarrassing to the cartel that amateurs are able to cause us problems. I can tell you, Sam, that I have already issued the order to kill. Only the details are open." Sam urged Max to make it soon.

Chapter

Chic was back home, ready for life to return to normal. He couldn't wait to get to work and set aside a little time to call Ann Renfro. He couldn't say if Ken was dead or alive, but he knew the location of the men who did. Ann would be delighted with this progress.

Ann answered on the second ring. "Hey, Chic, good news or bad?"

"Ann, I think I would call this good news. I haven't found Ken, but I have located the two guys who managed his boat, *Amedee*, for him. I'm positive that they know where he is."

"How on earth did you locate those guys, Chic?"

"We believe that Captain Hayes and Doug still work for the company that Ken worked for when he disappeared. I think the headquarters for the gang is located in Belize."

Chic and Suzy met with the Renfro family, and they all agreed that Chic would go to Belize to learn what he could from Doug and Captain Hayes. Chic, being a careful man, planned to leave for Belize as soon as possible but didn't disclose a date. He had already arranged for the equipment he needed; a boat, lodging, and the semiautomatic 9mm pistols would all be waiting for him. There was no point in delay. His plan was to pick up the boat at Livingston and motor to Fronteras, located on Lake Izabal. Chic also found that going into a town by boat worked well with the locals. They seemed to accept you more easily.

After the meeting, Myra drove home in her humble car, a Ford Taurus, looking as common as humble pie. As she entered the car, her conservative dress could not hide the hell cat within.

Myra left the family meeting itching to call her secret lover. Myra was a beautiful woman. She had jet-black hair and ice-green eyes, and at five feet nine, she cut a figure any model would die for. She worked as a model in New York as a young woman in her twenties. She was now a very young thirty-four. It was her brain, however, that propelled her to first in her class at Harvard.

It was at Harvard where she met a very talented and wealthy Larry Moses. He became the number-three man at BCWB, a large investment bank in Boston, partly because of his famous family but mainly because of his talent. His business acumen was recognized in business circles the world over. Larry was married with two children. He fit the profile of a family-loving conservative businessman. Unknown to his family, he had a dark side that only Myra understood. Myra was aware that Larry served on the executive committee at the bank with David Richburg and Gilman Loeb, the bank CEO.

Myra was the type of woman who scared the hell out of any normal guy. Smart, beautiful, savvy, she was the kind of woman no man could control. Her character was as overpowering as her mother's (Ann). She was very capable of choosing the male with whom she intended to satisfy her basic need for sexual gratification. She used and discarded men with great aplomb.

Her need for unusual sexual fulfillment, however, was reserved for Larry. The two of them meshed perfectly in their lust for the occult and perverse sexual experiences. They managed to lead what appeared to be normal lives except for a couple of rendezvous a year, when their demons within took control. When they met, they were driven into unfettered and uncontrollable passion. Boiling beneath their thin, civilized exterior was a heat that would warm the devil's heart if he had one.

Myra placed a call to Larry on a coded, encrypted line.

"Hello, my love, are you ready for your gift?"

"Yes, dear," Larry responded. "Will you be able to meet me in Tulum next week?"

"You bet. I will be there on the 11:00 a.m. flight to Cancun. Can you pick me up?"

"I will be waiting on you," he answered. "You did get the account I set up for you in Belize? I know Ken didn't express himself very well, but he was very grateful for your assisting him in company business. I know Ken wanted you to have his accounts. He was a valuable employee. We are sorry to lose him."

"Yes, thank you, love," Myra said. "Now, I have a special treat for you when we get there. I need to let you know how much I appreciate your looking after me. Now, there is something you need to know about my family. I told you Chic called and asked for a meeting with us and that we hired him to investigate Ken's disappearance." Myra gave Larry a full report of her mother's conversation with Chic.

"I understand that Chic plans to go to Belize soon and see what he can find out."

"Myra, don't worry. Chic is on our radar, and we do not intend to let him continue his investigation. We'll be waiting on him. Now we know you can handle your family. Don't be too obvious about your newfound wealth. What you and I know is between us. Our secret must be forever sealed."

"Don't worry, love," she assured him. "You keep my secrets, and I will keep yours. Our shared pleasures will remain our private nirvana."

"Hold that thought, beautiful, until we meet next week."

Myra also had work to do that night. She was wet with anticipation. She quickly changed into her hunting outfit: a short skirt, low-cut blouse, spiked high heels, and no underwear. She would reel in the selected man like a spent fish, tongue hanging out and panting like a dog. She picked her subjects carefully—tall, thin hips, long fingers, physically fit, with a slightly aggressive disposition. With that picture in mind, she pulled out of the driveway in her new red Porsche.

As she pulled out of her driveway, she had a fleeting thought of Ken. After the call to her secret lover, benefactor, and provider, Myra's spirits had soared. The rising RPM of the Porsche and the growing vibration of the ride reverberated through her body, driving her to a new height of sensual pleasure. She coasted back into dull reality, with her mind focused on the moment.

What is it about a little secret, a little deception … well, a big damned lie, she conceded, *that makes life so much more interesting?*

She had one more fleeting thought of Ken and some of the un-sisterly things they enjoyed together. Ken was a good man, but he was in her way. He was not in her class.

Now, all of the fruit of his labor was hers, and all she had to pay was the gift of sensual pleasure to a kindred spirit. She had earned it. What had her parents and brother done to earn it? Nothing. She, on the other hand, was part of a large enterprise, which gave her a lot of pride. She was the one who made it possible for Ken to make his money.

Past pleasures, promises, and recent potentials faded as she gunned the Porsche to her next hunting ground. She had an immediate itch. She did, after all, need to warm up her techniques for Larry.

Myra knew she was invited to Belize not just as a play toy for Larry but because she had contacts in Amsterdam with people who had connections to the Russians. She would be able to broker substantial deposits for the banking interest of the enterprise in Belize. She had gained valuable information about manipulation of foreign currencies. Yes, she was confident that she would become indispensable.

Chapter

10

Heath and Chic met at Joe and Eddy's for breakfast, a routine they had established whenever they both were in town. Suzy and Mary, Heath's girlfriend, were not big on getting up at seven on Saturday morning just to have breakfast at Joe and Eddy's. This was purely a guys' thing. Heath and Chic ordered their usual deluxe breakfast.—Heath's over light, and Chic's scrambled.

"How was your trip to Sand Mountain, Chic? Did you find any useful information?"

"I actually did find some very useful information from Suzy's cousin, Buck, the one that took me to a cockfight. To get this straight, Buck took me to the cockfight to meet his friend Jack, who knows Doug. Doug was one of the crew, along with Captain Bart Hayes, who operated the *Amedee* for Ken Renfro. The *Amedee*, as you recall, disappeared at about the same time as Ken. I found out that Doug and Captain Bart work on a motor yacht located in Lake Izabal, in Guatemala. This is a very isolated place. There is a small town called Fronteras where the lone southbound highway out of Yucatan crosses Lake Izabal. We believe that Doug and Captain Hayes still work for the same company they were with in Florida. They should be a treasure trove of information."

"Chic, that's a long way out of my jurisdiction. You would need the FBI or DEA to penetrate in Belize, Mexico, or that general area. What's your plan?"

"The short version is, Heath, I don't have one. That's where I need some help. In terms of our actually having hard evidence of Rico violations, we stand empty-handed. What I have in mind is to reassemble all the information we have gathered about the business dealings of Ken's companies and let Suzy and her friend Nancy analyze the data. Nancy is a professor and is retired from Wall Street. She knows the mortgage business better than anyone I know. If any patterns can be gleaned from the information, they can do it. Then we need to continue to check out George, Ken's replacement in operations here in Pensacola, under the theory that he's somehow involved with the same group as Ken and Victor. We are fairly certain that while all the players on the money-laundering side were killed in this area, the drug part of their business is still active in the Panhandle."

"I assume, Chic, that you want me to turn my information over to Suzy to add to your pool of information?"

"Yes. Aside from the fact that those two ladies are good at this, I need to keep Suzy's mind busy while I head to Guatemala. I'm going to need some help, Heath. I need some first-rate listening devices and probably a partner who can fit in as a local. This would be a free working vacation. Fishing will be a part of our disguise."

"Chic, you know the department doesn't have the money to pay for that kind of thing."

"Yeah, I know. I talked to Ken's family, and they agreed to cover the cost. I got a chance to talk to the family in Tennessee as part of my trip to Sand Mountain. I was very impressed with his family. His mother is a retired nurse, his father a family doctor, his sister is a professor at Vanderbilt, and his brother is a neurosurgeon. Makes you wonder how Ken got off on the wrong path in life."

"Yeah, Chic, some people just don't have any reason to be the crooks they are. Ken was obviously successful at what he did. He had the brains, personality, and drive to be successful at any line of work he chose. A loss of a potentially good man to the evil forces."

"Well, the family has no idea what has happened to Ken. They have not heard from him. Perhaps more telling is that they don't know enough about his business to give me any leads. Ken was as good at hiding information from his family as he was in deceiving me. They've not received a Christmas card, birthday card, or gift, which he normally would send. So, the fact that I have located the guy who knows where he probably is was exciting to them. They have agreed to take care of the cost."

"It is strange that their kind of family has had no contact with Ken," said Heath. "Even his vast wealth evaporated into foreclosure. How do we explain that?"

"Actually, that was a brilliant move on Ken's part or on the part of his employer. I think that Ken is the guy who actually devised the overall scheme of daisy chain corporations as well as other tools to hide his tracks. For example, had he left titles to all his assets in his name or in the name of his corporation when he left the country, his assets would remain here and be subject to probate. If he turned up dead, then there could be substantial litigation, which would eventually involve his bosses. They couldn't allow that to happen. By putting mortgages on all the real and personal property at a very low ratio of debt to value, he could simply draw that money down after leaving the country. The mortgage holders would then take the property. This could be done in a way that we would never penetrate to the core.

"The family has money, and they will spend some to find out if Ken is dead or alive."

"So, Chic, I take it that you're going down to Lake Izabal and that area to fish and see what you can find out. I take it you want the listening devices to see if you can pick up any conversations on the yacht."

"Yes. I'll be on the plane in the morning headed toward Belize. I'll give you a call along the way."

"I see the waitress coming with our breakfast. What time are we to meet the guys at the city golf course?"

"I told them we'd be there at 9:30," said Heath. "That should give us time to be ready to tee off at 10:00. I hope we both can get our heads out of our butts and play some golf today. Last time, we were a little discombobulated."

"Don't worry, Heath. I'm ready to show those guys what the real Chic can do. I've been practicing, you know."

And so the pressing problems of the world melted away as the two stout-hearted men prepared for war with a little white ball.

Larry Moses was careful to follow set procedure. The Boston triad knew the value of procedure. It was designed to provide an impenetrable firewall between the banking side of the business, the enforcement side, and operations. The wall between the legal aspects of the business and the side that raised the money would decide which money had to be laundered and what transactions had to remain inviolate. Extreme discipline by all the men in responsible positions was required. Strict rules had to be followed to maintain the relationship along the daisy chain of the corporations to make them work in perfect harmony. Only the top management in the enterprise could be privy to the entire picture; only they knew the true nexus of the tiered structure. Keeping all the parts operating like a finely tuned transmission was Larry's primary job.

The responsibility was enormous. It did not please Larry that he was called upon to make life-and-death decisions. On the other hand, he recognized that if it was his life or someone else's life, he had no problem resolving the issue in his favor. Bringing order to a naturally chaotic enterprise required an artist with lethal powers.

Larry had received a call from Myra informing him that Chic and Suzy met with their family and that Chic was going to Lake Izabal in the next day or two. Action was required. Fortunately, the banking side of the operation was in Boston. Gilman Loeb was the chief operating officer of BCWB. Larry was in the investment operations department, and David Richburg was the chief compliance officer.

All three of these men were on the executive committee of the board and were thereby involved in world operations. From their lofty position, the Sinaloa cartel had a powerful investment wing. Based on Larry's information about Chic, they met at their usual place, which was the bank's fifty-foot fishing boat. This boat was kept strictly for the executive committee. It was equipped with a secure room where their calls and communications could not be monitored.

Larry got Max on the speakerphone, and the meeting began. Larry repeated the information he had received from Myra.

David, known for his personal hate for Chic, spoke first. "Guys, let's go ahead and take Chic out. Why wait?"

"Max, don't we already have plans to take out Hayes and Doug in Lake Izabal?"

"Sure do," reported Max. "Looks like Chic is making it easy to kill several birds with one stone. Do we all agree to put him on our list?" All agreed. "Okay, men, I've got work to do. I'll be in touch."

The meeting adjourned to Miller time. "So, Larry, how do you handle Myra? I didn't think you were man enough to handle that firebrand."

"Hell, David, I do a better job than you do with Doll. At least Myra's not sweet on Chic."

David, known for his temper, flashed red in the face and made a hostile move toward Larry.

"Okay, kids, cool it." Gilman separated the men long enough to cool down the situation.

"Look, guys, that damn Chic has made a religious nutcase out of Doll. And she has closed her legs to me. Hell, I think they've been carrying on since college." David clearly had lost his control.

"That's a hell of a note, David." Gilman put his arm around David and said, "Look, if Max fails to kill Chic, he's yours. Take him out any way you want."

"Thanks, Gilman."

Chapter

11

Chic gazed out the window of the puddle hopper as it banked left over Belize City. Soon, the urban sprawl gave way to the pristine and expansive jungles that were once home to the Mayan. He wondered what it would be like to get lost down there, to be all alone with the zillions of biting insects, cockroaches the size of small dogs, and all kinds of nasty snakes. He felt a shiver run through him, and he tried to think of something else. He'd be at Lake Izabal in no time, where he'd stake out the yacht. His friend Heath had set him up with some powerful unidirectional receivers that could pick up conversations from four hundred yards. Heath had also set him up with Danny, who was seated next to him. Danny was a detective and might come in handy in case things went sideways. Danny was from Honduras, and he would feel right at home in a Spanish-speaking country.

Heath lined up the necessary permission for Danny to go with Chic to Belize and then onto Fronteras. Chic and Danny arrived in Livingston without incident. They picked up a twenty-eight-foot fishing boat designed for use in local waters. The draft was shallow enough to cross the sandbar without using a tipping procedure. They were dressed for the part. Danny was the guide. Chic was the fisherman looking for a local fishing experience.

They checked out the boat and supplies prepared for them by Danny's cousin, a local who grew up within fifty miles of this spot. Heath made the arrangements, including the sidearms they needed. It was too late to leave Livingston, so they spent Friday night there. Early Saturday morning, they headed up river to Fronteras, which would be their base for operations. They arrived at the Portugal Hotel and Marina just before dusk.

The hotel was very nice. It was like something out of an old Tarzan movie—big deck on the water connected to the bar, all open to Mother Nature. The food was excellent, especially the seafood. Service was with a smile. The water view, the jungle, and the big tropical flowers were everywhere. This natural beauty was, in Chic's eyes, a gift from God. Such beauty should not be defiled by the dark nature of his task at hand.

Chic and Danny sat on the open deck sipping one of those marvelous rum drinks so popular in the Caribbean. They remained silent as they watched the setting sun clothe everything in that special shade of pink only seen in the tropics.

Chic had never watched the sunset like this without a certain sadness. The world had experienced a glorious sunrise, and he had experienced a busy day on the river that unfolded in one beautiful scene after another. But now the day was dying, leaving a sadness in his soul at the gradual loss of light. Chic always wondered how he managed to feel such joy and sadness at the same time. As soon as the sun withdrew its unmatched colors of sundown, night appeared and lifted the shroud of sadness briefly. The transformation washed the night in the mystery that the stars and deep darkness bestowed.

What could he say? The transition from light to dark had made him sad since he was a child. At sea or on the water at sunset, a shot of cognac soothed the melancholy within his soul. Chic was not a drinking man, but he did make this one exception. In his training as practicing clinical psychologist, Chic had studied these particular reactions as well as other quirks in his own personality. He first noticed this reaction on road trips with his family. He discovered he just didn't like sunset. He had no problem with nighttime, but it was the transition to darkness that plucked on his psyche.

On Friday, Chic and Danny sat on the beach in Livingston silently observing the heavens tell the glory of God. Observing the heavens was one of Chic's favorite activities at night.

Meanwhile, Captain Hayes and Doug were making plans to go see a little cockfighting in El Estor. The captain didn't like anyone getting too close to the yacht, so they anchored *Angel* three miles south of the small village in the northwest corner of Lake Izabal, taking the dinghy to shore. They had received instructions to stay on board and not to venture into Fronteras, but the captain didn't see any real harm in going ashore to El Estor.

The first mate, Roberto, was a competent sailor and could handle *Angel* if any problems developed. Doug, who acted as a second in command on the *Amedee*, was not qualified as chief master. On *Angel*, he was the second engineer. It was the first mate who suggested the captain needed a little diversion. It was he who said the local ladies were very interesting. The hook had been baited, and the captain bit. Who could blame him?

The hard-bottomed Zodiac complemented the forty-meter yacht. El Estor hardly deserved anything like this. Doug was at the helm and did a fine job of pulling the craft up on the beach. He finished the job by attaching a heavy chain through the motor mounts, through the helm, and finally through an eyelet on the bow of the dinghy. He looped the chain to a secure stanchion and doubled back to another eyelet on the Zodiac. He removed a few critical breakers, which rendered the motor inoperable.

"Good job, Doug," said Hayes.

"Captain," said Doug, "you really think this town is big enough to have a whorehouse?"

"Don't you worry, Doug. Every town here has a church, a whorehouse, and somebody selling some drug or something that will blow your mind."

"Where's the cockfighting arena?" asked Doug.

"It's not far from here. It's a metal building behind the soccer field. When we get back tonight, we'll need to pull anchor and relocate. We don't want to give the thieves around here any bright ideas. We look like an inviting target."

"Captain, we've got some boys on board that would love nothing better than a little gunplay," said Doug. "They're sitting on the dock right now just looking for an opportunity to engage in a little target shooting."

"Good thought," Hayes replied. "Remind me to get them on the radio before we head back out tonight. If they get too drunk, we might be the target."

Doug and the captain stopped at a cantina across the street from the cockfighting arena, had a couple of drinks, and gathered a little local information. It was a rough bunch of local thugs, drinking, cursing, and playing a special brand of checkers that the natives loved.

Captain Hayes had learned better than to think he could beat the locals at checkers. It seemed like every town had its own version of checkers, and it became more fluid as the game progressed. They particularly loved to take a gringo's money for a spin. Playing against a stacked deck would only be charity.

The captain hung around long enough to find out the local rules of the cockfight. There were always special circumstances and special people that required special attention. You could bet your last dollar that screwing the gringo was the high spot of these cockfights.

It didn't take long to get into the spirit of the game. Doug lost $150, and the captain won $225. Not bad to make that much off those broke half-assed thugs.

The best thing to come out of the cockfight, other than some local brew, was information on the best whorehouse in town. The captain was concerned that the locals suggested a different house than was recommended by the first mate. After talking to several locals, the captain was convinced the first mate had given him bad advice. A couple of the top dudes were headed to the choice spot, so all the captain had to do was follow. If the place was good enough for these boys, it was good enough for him.

The house turned out to be a rundown old place, but the sheets were clean. More importantly, the girls were young, pretty, and willing. The captain cracked a little smile at the wisdom of this little side trip to heaven.

He caught the eye of a lovely young thing who couldn't have been more than sixteen. She could rival his sweetie on the ship. Maybe, he thought, he could talk her into coming back with them on the boat. She could entertain the whole crew.

The captain and Doug managed to raise hell until about two in the morning. At that point, they had expended all of the energy they possessed. Doug was a little pissed when the captain tapped him on the shoulder in the middle of a passionate embrace. He reminded him that he had to handle the dinghy going back to the boat.

"Get your pants on, you stupid shit," bellowed the captain. "Go on down to the dock and check on the boat, check in with the first mate, and come back and let me know when we're ready to leave. As captain, I'm entitled to one last shot at that sweet little thing."

"Crap," Doug grumbled under his breath. "I get all the shit jobs."

When he leaned over to pull up his pants, he fell forward, hitting his head on the wall. He realized he was almost too shitfaced to handle the Zodiac. Doug stumbled out of the door, hoping he had enough strength left to push the dinghy back into the water.

Doug managed to get to the Zodiac, pull in the chain, and replace the breakers. He got the boat into the water and reattached the chain to make sure the vessel didn't float off. Doug decided that, even drunk, he was a better sailor than were most men. The captain was lucky to have him.

———————•———————

He did not see two men who were hiding behind a dark shed, silently watching every move he was making. Jose and Miguel had been dropped off earlier in the night about a mile up the beach, so they could work their way into position. They planned carefully to complete the task in a way that would never be discovered. There would be no trace of two human bodies after this night. These men were not concerned with the loss to this world, nor the character of two human souls, if in fact the soul existed.

They had been stationed in another town waiting for the call that would let them know when the captain and Doug left *Angel*. Plans had already been made for the place where the bodies would be buried. They would complete the job, return the Zodiac to the ship, and then disembark at Livingston.

They lay patiently in wait for the captain and Doug to stagger toward the Zodiac. The targets sounded like two demons who had just escaped from hell. They waited until both men were in the Zodiac and the motor started. At that moment, Miguel got himself and Jose into position. Two seven-millimeter hollow-point bullets fired from two silenced rifles pierced Doug and the captain in their heads. Death was instant. The shooters were pleased they had dropped both men in the boat, certainly saving a lot of effort. It was going to be hard enough to move them from the boat to their final resting place.

Miguel and Jose walked to the Zodiac, shoved it into the water, and headed into the night. Miguel directed Jose to take the helm, and he would direct them to a secret cove on the opposite side of the lake where preparations had been made for the bodies. It took a lot of effort to haul the dead men out of the Zodiac and drag the cadavers fifty feet into the deep grave they had prepared earlier. They extracted the gold-capped teeth with the usual method, using a heavy metal hammer. Their money, gold necklaces, and rings were confiscated; all metal was removed. Then acid was poured onto the bodies and allowed to do its magic. When the two men were satisfied that the bodies were essentially destroyed, they covered the bodies with lye, and the grave was covered. Thick vegetation was carefully laid out over the area.

The two bodies had been stripped of all possible identification. Their clothes and billfolds were burned. When they left in the Zodiac, this part of the jungle looked as though it had been untouched by human hands. They tossed the stripped teeth into the water as they navigated the Zodiac to the yacht. As soon as they arrived at *Angel*, her anchor was lifted, and she headed toward the Gulf of Mexico. The first mate of *Angel*, Roberto, was now the captain. The situation at Lake Izabal was completed, or so they thought.

The first mate timed his speed so he would arrive at Fronteras between three thirty and four on Sunday morning. The passage of a forty-meter yacht in these waters would not go totally unnoticed, but the timing should reduce it to a minimum.

Jose and Miguel arrived at *Angel* expecting to leave the area but instead were instructed to leave the dinghy tied up. They were directed to Captain Roberto's quarters. "Gentlemen, I have received orders that you are to remain here and take out two guys who are investigating us. Here's a copy of their recent photographs. They are in Fronteras, so you should have no problem finding them. When you finish the job, we'll make arrangements to pick you up." After a general discussion, the men were sent back to the dinghy. They were not happy, but they knew complaints were dangerous.

Chic and Danny had no illusion this was going to be easy. They did expect, however, to be able to locate a rather large yacht in the area of Lake Izabal. A yacht this size would have to be specifically designed to get over the sandbar at the mouth of the river. The yacht would be a real novelty and a topic of conversation among locals.

Chic and Danny sat in the restaurant taking in an excellent view of the river, bridge, and local marina in the way law enforcement officers would. It was that general demeanor that alerted the cockroaches of the world that someone was an immediate and present danger to them. To the professional crook, a lawman, in or out of uniform, reeked of danger. Some egotistical officers believed this was the very aura that attracted women.

"How do you like the pancakes with bananas?" Danny asked at breakfast. "They are my favorite food in this world."

"Danny, I have to admit that I thought you were nuts when you suggested this, but they're marvelous," was the reply.

"The small bananas are outstanding, and they are 100 percent better down here where they're fresh and ripen on the trees. I've never found them to be this good in the States. You'll find that you have to come down here to get the really good stuff. Before we leave, we'll get some fruit like you've never tasted," Danny said.

"Chic, do you have a plan on how we should proceed this morning?"

"My plan is called basic snooping," said Chic. They managed to get a couple of steps before one of the local sleazebags approached them with a deal. The man had wet slick hair, big teeth, and a crooked smile. He began his pitch with a great deal on a Rolex watch. That didn't work, so he tried girls. Next he moved on to a selection of drugs. Chic finally took the man by the arm, took him a little bit to the side, and told him that they were narcs and if he did not shut up and get out of there, they were going to arrest him. The sleazebag disappeared quickly.

After ridding themselves of Slick, they managed to get to the manager of the hotel, who directed them to the unofficial harbor master in the area. This man had no official legal authority, but the harbor masters generally set the rules in the marina communities around the Caribbean. The hotel manager proved to be a rather observant kind of guy. He kept a close eye on the water traffic. It was part of his duties, he said, to operate the wet slips at the hotel. He was well aware of the large yacht and identified it as the *Angel*. He also noted that there was a corporate name and trademark on the yacht, but he was unable to provide specific information. As Chic expected, he was impressed with the big boat. It was the largest one the hotel manager recalled ever coming through Fronteras. He heard it had some kind of special flotation device that raised the boat high enough out of the water to cross the sandbar. He had not seen it in a couple of months. He had heard it was anchored somewhere in Lake Izabal, but he did not know where.

The harbor master was located about three blocks from the hotel. Chic had already found out that the harbor master's name was George, along with unsolicited information about what kind of an ass he could be. Fortunately, Danny and Chic didn't need anything official from George. This was a social visit, more or less.

Danny took the lead and introduced himself to the young lady who appeared to be George's secretary. They were invited to take a seat. George was sitting back in his chair, tilted to the maximum angle. His feet were on the desk, coffee and doughnut in his hands. His desk was in disarray. With all his power in this very small place, his general appearance was sloppy. His cowboy boots looked like they had never been polished. He was in a uniform that had not been pressed. The harbor master took a couple of calls while they waited for him to acknowledge their presence. He was irritated that he had to put down his coffee cup to speak on the phone. George eventually looked in the direction of Danny and Chic, lowered his feet from the desk, adjusted his baseball cap, and barked in their direction.

"What you guys here for?" he said in broken English.

"Sir," said Danny, "we are here fishing for a few days, and we wanted to check in with you and make sure we're okay to do that. My name is Danny, and this is Chic. I always like to clear in with the harbor master."

"You're a very smart man, Mr. Danny," said George. "Most people don't understand that they need to keep me happy. You boys are clear. Just make sure if you have any problem, you check in with me. I'm the guy keeping things moving around here."

"Thank you, sir," said Danny with his best posture that said, "I'm the little guy, and you're the boss."

"Danny, you can call me George if you like. All my friends do."

After a minute of chatter about what his office did and discussing the functions of a harbor master in Central America, Danny sensed that he could open up with George about his real line of work.

"George," he began, "Chic and I are here fishing on vacation, but we both also work for the Pensacola Florida Sheriff's Office. I'm a full-time detective, and Chic is a clinical psychologist. Let me show you my badge."

Danny and Chic both presented their badges to George.

"Well, hell," was the response from the harbor master. "Who are you guys investigating down here?"

"We really aren't on official business," said Danny. "Somebody at the hotel where we're staying mentioned that there was a big forty-meter yacht in Fronteras named *Angel*. It just so happens that I was investigating such a yacht in Pensacola that caused a lot of damage at the local marina and left a big bill for damages. I didn't think I would ever see that boat again. Now it would be a gift from heaven if that yacht showed up down here in port at Lake Izabal where I just happened to be fishing. I need a few words with *Angel*'s captain."

"Son, I'd say you're the luckiest and unluckiest guy I have ever met," said George. "I was told by the people at the marina that *Angel* came through here headed east toward the gulf about four this morning. By now, they're long gone."

"Well, if it weren't for bad luck," Chic said, "we would not have any luck at all, George. Do boats have to report to you when they come and go? Do you have any information that might help us find them?"

"If they're going to stay here, then they would need to check in with me," George answered. "But they only passed by here and headed for the western part of Lake Izabal. We did record their name as *Angel* and the owner's name as Echeneis. Both names are a little stupid in my opinion."

"Marie," he said to his secretary, "did you hear anything about that yacht *Angel*?"

"Not really, boss," she said. "If I remember right, the captain's name was Captain Hayes. At least that's the way he reported it on the ship-to-shore radio transmission. Some of the guys said on the way out this morning they picked up some radio communication between a Captain Roberto with somebody. It was about a Captain Hayes and a crewmember embarking from Fronteras. That's about it."

"We appreciate that information," said Chic. "At least we now know the *Angel* is located in the western Caribbean. If the sheriff is interested in following up on it, that will be up to him. Today we are going to enjoy the rest of our vacation. There is fishing to do and good food to eat. We will let somebody else take care of the world's problems this week."

They shook hands, and while going out of the door, George gave them the names of a couple of his favorite places to eat.

"Okay, Danny," Chic said, when they got clear of anyone hearing the exchange, "as an experienced lawman, what do you think the chances are of that yacht leaving Lake Izabal the very day we arrive, and the two people we're looking for are no longer on the ship?"

"The odds of it being pure luck are nil," replied the detective.

"Only a very few people knew about our trip, and even fewer knew the purpose," Chic continued. "It is very hard for me to believe someone double-crossed me on this. I really would like to believe it was pure chance, but my brain tells me differently. Boston was warned about our mission here."

"Let's look at it this way, Chic," Danny replied. "If the *Angel* was still here, what could we find out that we don't already know?"

"That's a good question," said Chic. "If any of them were still here, we would get a picture of the boat as well as the owner's name. We already have the name of the probable owner, which will help us for sure. We can assume that Captain Hayes and Doug are dead. No big problem to our investigation since we didn't anticipate we would get to talk to them anyway. We do have the name of the new captain. All we lost is the opportunity to photograph the crew of Echeneis and maybe pick up information with our other equipment. My strong belief is that Ken, Captain Hayes, and Doug are all dead. We can't prove it, but based on history, I believe they would have left them on the *Angel* if they intended for them to live. A search of this area, even if we could pull that off, would be a waste of time. What information we can dig up from locals is still valuable to us.

"I think we got here quicker than they anticipated. Knowing now that there is a new captain and that the other two guys are gone is solid information."

"I agree," said Danny. "Knowing the name of the owner of the yacht will allow us to obtain more details, and it may be the only hard evidence we're going to need to find a solid lead to identify the criminal syndicate."

"Well, then we could drop our front and just act like the snoopy detectives that we are," said Chic. "What really bothers me is our need to identify the person leaking information to Boston. If it's not someone close to me or you, that only leaves the Renfro family. It's possible that they accidentally spilled the beans to someone else. If I believe that, then I have to assume Boston is keeping a close eye on the Renfro family. Otherwise, this information could not have filtered to Boston this quickly. One thing for sure, Captain Hayes and Doug were probably killed to keep us from getting to them or even taking a photograph."

Chic had a bad feeling about this. Is Suzy in danger? What should he do with the Renfro family? Should he call Suzy and warn her to stay alert? Chic finally concluded that it was not time to call home and warn everybody, at least not yet. In fact, who would he warn? There was only one member he could identify who could be involved with the Boston crime bosses. What really bothered him was Boston might actually get word of his warning. Ideally, he had to get home and do his investigating. He couldn't trust the Renfros, so it was probably better not to warn them. He and Danny would stay one more day and spend the rest of the day talking to the people on the waterfront there in Fronteras to see if they knew any more about the *Angel* and her crew.

So they took off on the south side of the river until noon. After noon, they covered the north side. Danny led the way with his Spanish, although what he spoke was not classical Spanish. By day's end, the two tired puppies once again sat on the veranda of the hotel.

In its way, it was a grand place—a combination bar and *palapa*. Throughout the Caribbean, a palapa is a place where all the sailors gather to tell their tall tales. To a guy like Chic, it was a marvelous opportunity to study human nature. The history of the nautical orator was not lost on this crowd. Central casting in Hollywood couldn't match the cast of characters seated on this deck. Many times Chic kicked himself for not taking a recording device to the verandas and around the marinas. He often considered gathering from his memories the stories for a book. He recognized, however, that the narratives of the sea and the islands were full of life in that environment when recited by real sea captains. The accounts and legends would probably fall flat in print.

The usual suspects were present and accounted for. The New York lawyer who claimed his sailboat originally belonged to Earl Flynn. Then there was a sail maker who built his own boat while living with his wife and three kids in Seattle, Washington. He told his family he was going sailing for a long weekend and never returned. There were a couple of retired teachers who got tired of watching their friends check out of this life, one by one. They wanted to enjoy life a little before they died. They sold all their worldly goods, bought a boat, and had been here living the good life ever since. There was the wealthy couple, who one day simply chose to live this way rather than play at "normal" life. Once in a while, they would fly home to see their kids, but overall, they were indistinguishable from all the other marine nomads. The drunken sailor with a peg leg and parrot along with a crowd of unidentifiable people completed the picture.

Chic had always been at ease with people of this breed. The well-to-do couple that lived on a boat was well adjusted with a firm understanding of their place in the universe. Living at sea had a way of humbling the most arrogant. He couldn't help but notice that the older couple was in excellent physical condition. Climbing around a boat, large or small, does make the body trim and flexible.

Everybody at this palapa had a real, deep life story to tell, some tragic, some inspiring. All of the stories were spellbinding.

As usual, Chic warmed up quickly to the gathering. Eventually, he felt comfortable enough to tell a few of his own favorite yarns. He began with his adventures in Maya Cay.

"Some of you fellows probably remember an island just north of Belize City called Maya Cay," he said.

"You bet," growled a black-bearded sailor leaning against the rail. "Maya Cay, yes. In fact, I met the prettiest girl I ever saw there. Man, I thought I was in love until I picked up a paper one morning, and there she was, right on the front page, arrested for doing certain unmentionable acts in a public park."

A lady sailor looked up at Black Beard and with dazed eyes said, "You're so damned ugly she wouldn't even sell you any."

"Okay, children," said Chic, "you keep this up, and I'll have you all singing 'Kumbaya' together."

The crowd snickered, amazingly, in unison. Their eyes spoke the same language: *who in hell is this asshole?*

"Well, if you know the island, then you know it was an old Mayan burial ground. In Belize, a man with a gun is usually to be feared. About two in the morning, a man came out of the woods and told me he was guarding the island. He said there used to be evil spirits here, but he killed them all. I asked the guard, whose name was Ling, how he was able to kill the evil spirits.

"Ling told me his mother was a shaman, and it was she who taught him how to kill the evil spirits. He then went through the entire ritual with me. 'First,' he said, 'you rub your clothes with garlic. Then you rub your hands and face. Then you rub the shotgun shells and the gun. Then you put on a necklace of garlic.' He then mumbled some magic words and pronounced he was ready. He explained how he would go out and wait until the spirits called his name: 'Liiinnnggg! Liiinnnggg! Liiinnnggg!'

"'I would then shoot them,' said Mr. Ling.

"Mr. Ling told me it took him about a month, but he eventually killed all the evil spirits. He told me it was then safe on the island.

"While Mr. Ling was dead serious, I couldn't help but recall the trade winds blowing through the dead prawns on the trees, which produces a zinging sound. Mr. Ling might believe that the spirits were calling him: 'Liiinnnggg! Liiinnnggg!'"

"Yeah, man," said Black Beard. "Strange shit happens in the jungle."

Danny spoke up. "By the way, we heard that there was a big forty-meter yacht anchored somewhere in Lake Izabal. Have any of you seen it? Its name is *Angel*."

"Yeah," said the retired teacher. "I saw it when it came through, but it didn't stop here. I don't believe the captain ever came ashore in Fronteras. At least I never saw him. I heard every now and again they would have a meeting on the boat. One or two times I saw a helicopter headed out toward the lake. I heard various people would fly in here and then be flown out to the boat."

"From what I heard," said Black Beard, "that was a real bunch of bastards on that boat. Never talked to us locals."

What Chic and Danny heard simply confirmed what they had heard all day. The only useful information was that no one had heard that Captain Hayes and Doug had departed the boat or that it had passed through Fronteras, headed for the gulf.

Chic and Danny decided the next day they would explore Lake Izabal and see what they could see. Fronteras to El Estor at the western end of the lake was approximately twenty-five miles. They could easily make the trip in a day.

Chic had especially liked the retired couple from Florida. They had to be in their late sixties or early seventies, but life had made them look like a pair of forty-year-old athletes. The man had his story about how he was rich, as rich as the richest man on earth. He said he had the one thing the rich man didn't have. Chic took the bait and asked the old sailor, "And what would that be?"

"Happiness, son," said the old man. "When was the last time you met a happy rich man?"

"Well," said Chic, "I don't have an answer for that right off the top of my head. I'm going to have to think about it."

Later that night, Chic lay in bed pondering the day's activities. The old man's words kept coming back to him. What about the men who ran the grand criminal enterprise he was investigating? They had to be rich men. So, what exactly was their motivation? How much money, toys, and power were needed to satisfy their greed?

Chapter

12

At 6:00 a.m. Chic and Danny were eating breakfast. They were on their way by seven. They took their time, checking out the interesting foliage on shore along the way. They didn't expect to see anything relevant to the investigation, but you never know. They pulled into the peer in El Estor at eleven thirty. Since El Estor was the only populated area beyond Fronteras, it seemed reasonable that if the crew of the *Angel* came ashore, it would be in this isolated place.

It was a crappy little place. The people were friendly enough, but it was simply a small, remote village with a couple of open-air places to eat.

Chic knew from experience in Central and South America that the best and safest food was at the outdoor vendors. Here you could see your food being prepared and cooked. The beef stew and rice were excellent. The vendor was more than happy to introduce the boys to the two local whorehouses. Every sailor confined to a boat for a long time will visit a local whorehouse at the first opportunity.

Chic and Danny picked the cleanest one to start with. The madam was most helpful. She retrieved a beautiful young girl, who could have been anywhere from fifteen to twenty-two years old to talk to Chic. The girl remembered the captain and his friend. She said he was a nice guy, treated her well, and gave her a big tip. She would be happy to have him back.

She said her little brother was down near the pier that night. He saw the two guys from the big yacht get shot. Two men were hiding in the dark, and as soon as the captain and the other guy were shot, they fell into their dinghy. The men took the dinghy and sped off with the bodies inside.

Chic had the girl get her brother, Pee Wee, who told the same story with a little more emotion. Pee Wee explained he was hiding in the dark, drinking beer. He was only twelve, so he knew he had to lay low. He also confessed that he smoked a little cigar. He was about to light up when he heard the shots. He showed Chic and Danny where he was hiding, where the shooters were, and where the dinghy was tied to the dock. He told them that they headed out across the lake without their lights on. Next morning, the big boat was gone.

Pee Wee made Chic promise not to tell his mother about any of this. Chic patted Pee Wee on the head, gave him ten dollars, and swore his secrets were safe.

"Danny, what's the chance of finding the bodies?" he said.

"Absolutely no chance. We may as well go back to the motel. We might even get a little fishing in tomorrow."

"You got it. There's no point in looking for Doug and the captain. They have gone to collect their great reward. Let's spend tomorrow fishing and then head back to Florida."

"You got it, boss."

———•———

As they walked down the street toward their boat, Chic noticed a rough-looking dude at an outside bar, trying not to be noticed. Chic couldn't really explain how a person trying not to be noticed in an open situation was, to the trained eye, waving a red flag. Chic nudged Danny's arm and without turning his head asked, "Did you notice that tough-looking guy at the bar on my left?" He's not a good guy. Did you bring your weapon?

"Yes, it's in my backpack secured in the boat locker," said Danny.

"Good. I have mine too, along with extra clips. We need to assume we're going to be attacked before we leave Lake Izabal."

They tried not to look too obvious about getting out of there, but their pace quickened. As they pulled away from the mooring, Chic saw the guy at the bar leave the area. Chic didn't like the way this guy looked or the way he was carrying himself. He exited the bar area like a man on a mission.

Chic told Danny to take the helm and he would retrieve their 9mm Glocks along with extra clips. Chic had no doubt that the killers were going to attack before they could get to safety, if there was such a place in this area of the world. Chic made ready for battle as much as one can be on a moving boat.

"You know, Danny, the fact the crooks could get these two killers in place this fast has to be through a leak. If that's not so, we got here in the middle of their planned operation to take out a couple of important witnesses. Had we been able to catch Doug and Captain Hayes, we may have been able to identify our true enemies. So, we show up, and the bosses get a chance to kill witnesses as well as the law men who are after them. Awfully convenient, don't you think?"

"Put it that way, Chic, and I'd say we better lock and load."

"I know one thing," Danny said with a crinkled brow. "You know these guys only have long guns, and we only have pistols. That is a clear advantage on their side. We'll have to find a way to get in close for a kill shot."

Chic said he was working on the problem. "I'll set up a protected area on what we think will be our firing position." Chic removed the seats and leaned them along each side of the boat. Life jackets were placed between the hull and the boards. Every loose board, box, and book was added to the mix. In the most likely defensive positions, he placed the tool boxes. As on most fishing boats, there was a fair supply of tool boxes to aid in this effort. Reflecting even one bullet could help save a life.

Aside from protection from the junk he found, Chic knew he was an excellent shot and was fairly certain Danny was also. He also brought along an adequate supply of 9mm ammunition and left all but a few rounds of hollow points behind. If they needed the hollow points, they each had one clip.

Chic also found that there was a 12-gauge shotgun on board to use to fire flares. This could become useful. Chic laid out the shotgun along with all the flares in the protected spot he had selected.

"What do you think, Danny? See any way we can improve on this?"

Danny carefully surveyed their firing position. His expression told it all. They were vulnerable, and this was going to be a fight to the finish. "Looks okay to me, Chic."

"The next question, Danny, is whether we should stay close to the shore where we can limit their approach and we can make a run for the shore, or go out to the middle of the lake. Which is better in your opinion?"

Both men went silent as they made their calculations. If they guessed wrong, it would be their last miscalculation.

Chis spoke up first. "I believe that close to the south shore is best. They can't follow us in on shore with a vehicle, so we won't be assaulted from land. It will have to be from the water. We can run to shore, get out, and use the boat as our barrier. They will eventually have to come closer to us, which will give us an advantage, as they'll be moving and we'll be firing from a stationary position. They'll either have to come to us or wait for another time."

"I agree. That's as good a plan as we can devise. It's better than running around in the open water."

"Great. Run toward the south shore and stay out about a hundred feet. The minute they start firing, let's move to shore and get out behind the boat, where they'll have to come within our firing range to get us."

The two assassins wasted no time. As soon as Chic and Danny left their mooring, Miguel and Lucas got to their boat and quickly left. Their assumption was that their target would head for the center of the lake and blast away at full speed. The assassins were no more than fifteen minutes behind their targets. They had sufficient speed to easily catch the fishing boat their targets were in.

The assassins actually passed Chic and Danny within twenty minutes of leaving the marine area.

Chic picked up the assassins in his binoculars as they sped by. Chic realized that the assassins had failed to consider that they might not be able to see an old fishing boat going along the shore backed up by verdant jungle. They could not easily see a slow boat. Chic's boat was not a shiny white boat and was not easily seen.

"Pull into the shore, Danny, and let's find a place to tie up the boat. If they find us, we'll be in a position behind the boat."

The assassins kept on for another fifteen minutes thinking the other boat was simply faster than they thought. They finally stopped their boat, drifting for a few minutes while they studied their situation. Now they realized their problem. They would have to backtrack along one side of the shore or the other. They couldn't do both sides at the same time. They couldn't go down the middle because then they wouldn't be able to see either shore. This was going to be more difficult than they thought.

The assassins decided to backtrack on the south side of the lake, purely because the south side was closer to them than the north side. After much thought, they decided to turn and go back west about a thousand feet from the south shore. If they didn't find the targets that way, they would simply have to go back to base and get them that night or the next day at their hotel. They reduced their speed to approximately fifteen knots where they could study the water to their north and shoreline to their left.

Chic found what was a perfect location as possible under these circumstances. They anchored the boat on shore, partially hidden by bushes and trees. The boat was pointed toward the open water. They actually were standing on a small, sandy knoll surrounded by water. They were protected by the boat and motor.

Thirty minutes later, Chic spotted the boat headed west back toward their area.

The assassins passed by them the first time. They came back in an easterly direction and finally spotted them. They could see the boat but not Chic and Danny. The assassins idled in the area with their bow pointed toward the shore.

Chic and Danny considered moving back into the jungle but decided the boat provided better protection.

The assassins decided to start firing from their present position. They let loose with a volley of twenty to twenty-five shots before they let up. They managed to shoot a few holes in the boat, but the engine protected them from any injury.

When the volley stopped, Chic was able to observe them close enough to realize they did not use a pair of binoculars. They were going to have to attack now or leave.

Miguel was behind the wheel, and Lucas was the shooter. Miguel gave full power headed toward Chic and Danny, and Lucas began firing with his rifle as they charged. At this point, it was too pistols versus one unsteady rifle. Miguel was headed directly at Chic's boat. When they got within a hundred feet of Chic and Danny, they seized their opportunity. They were able to quickly take Lucas out with a couple of body shots, using the hollow-head bullets. Miguel got in closer and made a hard right turn, swinging the boat sideways to Chic's boat.

At this point, Miguel was clearly in range and exposed.

All three shooters let loose with rapid volleys at about the same time. Miguel was taken down quickly but not before Danny took a shot in his left shoulder, and Chic was hit by shrapnel in the right temple. When the smoke cleared, Chic could see that Danny was shot in the shoulder area. Chic quickly got the first-aid kit from the barriers he had set up and went to work on Danny's shoulder. It took awhile, but he was able to stop the bleeding. It looked like some bone may have been clipped, but it appeared there were no body organs or vital parts damaged.

For Chic's part, a bandage took care of his problem until he could find time to check for foreign objects in the injured area of his forehead.

Chic made Danny as comfortable as he could, tied the assassins' boat to his boat, and headed back to Fronteras. The trip to Lake Izabal, Rio Dulce, and Fronteras was a disaster for Danny and Chic. They never expected that the crooks they were investigating would be waiting on them. A betrayal almost cost them their lives. It actually cost the lives of two of their witnesses, Doug and Captain Hayes. Two assassins were killed, and he and Danny were injured.

When they arrived in Fronteras, the two dead assassins had to be turned into the locals and of course the process that was required involved a lot of people and the State Department, and depending on the will of the local police, it could take days. Only through the intervention of the State Department, Heath, and other law enforcement officers were they able to get Chic and Danny released so they could get Danny home as quickly as possible for medical attention. Fortunately, Chic's injuries were not major, and Danny, after receiving some medical attention, was patched up enough to make the trip back home.

Suzy was going to be really upset about the gun battle and the fact that he received some injuries. Chic knew he should probably call, but he would see her within a few hours, and getting out of this area was the first priority.

Chic was deeply concerned that he had been the victim of the Renfro family at least twice. This one family, whom he thought so highly of in the beginning, was proving to be his nemesis. Was he losing his touch, or were they that good at deception? He reviewed everything he knew about Ken and his family, and even with hindsight, he couldn't put his finger on the demon.

Chapter

13

Papan and Izel, Sinaloa hit men, left their migrant hostile in Eufaula, Alabama, where they worked in a chicken-processing facility. Their cousin, Antonio, was also their boss who directed them to Anniston, Alabama, to do a job. They liked this assignment because they were going home after they completed the assignment.

Izel, always the nervous type, kept asking Papan, "You sure you know how to get to Anniston? How do you know? You ever been there before? How long is it gonna take?"

Finally, Papan had enough. "Shut your mouth, Izel. You don't need to know anything except when to make a shot and hit your target."

"Okay." He always let his brother know Papan was the boss. "I'll shut up. You just make sure we don't get lost. Are you sure Antonio wants us to go to Anniston?"

"I said, shut up. I'm in charge here. You just do what I tell you, and you'll be okay."

"Okay, okay." As usual, Izel had a sheepish look on his face.

"Izel, you know Antonio gave us this assignment as a favor so we can go back home. It's our turn. Antonio gave me the directions, and he's worked out all the details. None of that is your concern. Our job is to follow instructions. I'm the one who has the plan, so that is not your concern. You understand?"

"Yes, okay."

Papan was finally able to drive to the motel where they were staying in Anniston in relative peace. The next morning, on schedule, they met Antonio at 8:00 sharp. "Good morning, men. Hope you slept well."

"Yes, very well," said Papan, who was normally the spokesman for the two brothers. Izel was the shooter and was more reserved than his older brother. His job was to shoot, not talk.

"Eat up, guys. We have a couple of hours before I have to make my appointment," said Antonio.

The men didn't talk much during breakfast, but when they did, they spoke in English. They were well shaven and dressed in clean blue jeans and sporty shirts. When they finished their meal, they headed directly to their respective cars. Antonio was driving a Honda, and Papan was driving a Ford pickup with a camper on the back, which Izel could use as a shooting platform. They drove over to Quintard Mall where they parked. Antonio came over to the pickup truck to continue with his instructions.

"Now," instructed Antonio. "I will give you a sign when the target exits the beauty shop. Both of you watch for my signal between 10:00 a.m. and 10:30. Now take the camper over to the right position."

Papan was careful to park the camper truck into position, approximately three hundred feet from the beauty shop. He had the rear of the camper facing the target area.

Izel lined himself up in the camper, with the back hatch open, making sure he could see the target. He was now in position with his 9mm rifle and was ready to go.

"Izel, you be sure that I confirm the target. We can't make a mistake on that. Antonio will identify the target, but I'm the one who will tell you when to fire and take out the target."

"Okay, okay, Papan. I've got it. I'll wait for you. Okay? What time is it anyway?"

"You don't have to worry about the time. You just rest your little brain. Take a deep breath. You've got to make a good shot."

"Okay, okay."

At 10:40 a.m., Margie Beal came out of the beauty shop with a big smile on her face, obviously enjoying the beautiful day.

Antonio gave the signal.

"Izel. You see the target? She's the one who just came out of the door. The small lady, red hair and white blouse."

"Yes. I've got her."

"Fire at will," Papan instructed.

No one heard a sound. Margie simply collapsed to the ground, dead.

Without fanfare, Izel closed the camper rear gate, and Papan drove the camper from the scene and headed up I-20 toward the shopping center where the vehicle exchange would occur. At the next intersection, he exited to the right and entered the shopping center's parking lot. He found the Honda that he was to take. The keys were on top of the left front wheel. The keys to the truck were left in the truck's glove compartment. They got into the Honda, and in the glove compartment were their plane tickets for the 4:00 p.m. flight on Delta, along with passports and some cash. They also were left two carry-on bags where they could change clothes, leaving their old clothes in the carry-on bags. The rifle was hidden in a designated place in the camper. That very night, Papan and Izel were able to eat supper at their favorite restaurant in Isla Mujeres, Mexico.

———•—•———

Chic and Danny's flight back to Atlanta was very uncomfortable. Danny was in severe pain. Chic arranged for an ambulance to be waiting on him as soon as they landed in Atlanta. Heath would be there to debrief Danny and to make sure that he was properly cared for at the hospital. Then it was obvious to Chic that the criminal gang would not give up. At this point, the criminal enterprise had lost too many assets as a result of Chic's activities to be ignored. He and Suzy would both be high on their hit list. It was clear that he had to identify the crooks and beat them to the punch.

Suzy would take this very hard. Then she would have to be told about Danny, and she would see the bandages on his head. Suzy would probably be more disturbed that he had not called her from Belize and let her know that all of them were in real danger.

Chic knew he had to brace himself. As he had reminded himself many times, "Put on your big-boy britches."

It took Chic approximately seven hours to get out of Atlanta and drive home to Pensacola. As Chic got his bags out of the car and headed to his front door, he was physically and mentally wasted. Chic put his bags down, got his key, and opened the front door. He was shocked to see Suzy leaning against the wall with the phone in her hand, crying. Red alarm bells went off in his head.

Suzy collapsed into a chair next to the phone. Her sobbing became uncontrollable. All she could get out was, "My fault! My fault! Why Mother! Why did those bastards kill Mother?"

Chic grabbed her hand, knelt down, and attempted to give her someone to lean on. Suzy was not responding. She grew stiff and balled up into the fetal position. She dropped the phone and remained in the fetal position as Chic attempted to caress her. Suzy was clearly exhibiting an escape response from a present physical threat in her mind.

Eventually, Suzy allowed Chic to hold her, but her body remained stiff. All of her muscles were taut, and she was unable to respond verbally.

It took more than forty-five minutes to gain enough control to at least attempt to speak to Chic. She had not really noticed his presence and certainly had not noticed that his head was wrapped in a bandage.

Eventually, between sobs, she managed to get out, "Chic, those bastards killed Momma! Why would they do that? If they want to kill someone, kill me. It's all my fault anyway!" She then went back into that dark place in the mind where there is only fear and anger.

"Suzy, it's not your fault. Those demons did this to hurt you as much as they could. I'm here. I'll look after you. Don't fear."

"You can't help me, Chic," she continued in a distraught tone. "We're fighting a major cartel, just you and me. There is no hope. If I hadn't been acting like a cheap whore, we wouldn't be running for our lives."

Chic took some time, hugged her, rubbed her back, spoke softly into her ear, and then softly lifted her face to his. "But, love, you and I would never have met any other way. For me, all the risk in the world is worth the price. Please don't ever doubt that. God has a plan. We have to have the faith.

"Baby, there's no way I can remove the depth of the pain for your mother's loss. I can only imagine how I would feel if I lost you. It would be an unspeakable loss."

And so Chic continued to minister to Suzy's need. He continued to stroke her gently, and he gave her space as she needed it. Eventually even in life's worst circumstances, the pain gets gobbled up into all those necessary rituals the living have to do in these circumstances. When Suzy had quieted down enough to notice his head injury, Chic felt like he could assure her that he would talk to the sheriff in Anniston and make all the arrangements for the funeral.

The thought of the funeral set Suzy off again.

Chic was in a state of shock. He and Danny had barely escaped with their lives from Lake Izabal. He didn't find out about Margie's murder until he got home to Suzy. It blew Chic's mind that during the time he was flying back from Cancun to Atlanta, Margie had been murdered. Suzy and Chic's lives had been changed by this murder in a flash. The reality of the situation took time to sink in.

Chic was able to contact Heath, who was equally shocked by the events. But he agreed to dig up as much information as he could and call him on his cell.

Chic eventually got the location of Margie's body and the name of the funeral home.

The drive to Anniston was difficult. Suzy was still in total shock. If she could have relived her life and not had all these horrible experiences, she would have gladly done it.

Perhaps it was the quietness of the car ride, or maybe the inner strength she felt sitting next to Chic, with his arm around her, that helped the fog lift a little bit. Suzy realized that she and Chic were now in a fight for life. Finally, Chic decided that Suzy was far enough along for him to tell her the rest of the story of Lake Izabal.

"Sweetheart, I didn't expect them to come after your mother or my family either. I guess I should've told you earlier, but the two guys I was looking for at Lake Izabal, Doug and Captain Hayes, were also killed. We found this out by pure chance. The yacht we were looking for left the first night we were there. I really didn't see any reason to disturb you about that because it didn't seem to pose a threat to you.

"Then after we left the small town where we found out about the murder of Doug and Captain Hayes, the same killers came after me and Danny. We managed to kill them both, but Danny was shot in the shoulder, and I got splinters and stuff in my head. That's the reason for my bandage.

"I hate to put all this on you, but you have to know the full extent of our danger. I should have called you from Belize, but I got bogged down in my own problems. Will you forgive me?"

Suzy sat back for a while, thinking. *What do you do? Grieve for Momma? Stew in my own fear? Thank God that Chic wasn't killed? Flail away at the darkness?*

"Of course I forgive you. Really, Chic, I have no idea what I would do without you. I hope you don't mind if I just don't talk for a while. The pain of the loss of my mother along with the threat to my life and yours … I must decide alone if I have the strength to stand by your side."

It took awhile, but Suzy finally accepted that her mother had left her in body only. She was with God, and Suzy believed that her mother's spirit was still present. Why would anyone, she thought, believe that a soul could be destroyed? Nothing else God has created can be destroyed. Suzy's anger was mollified by her belief that the soul is eternal and at the appointed time she would join her mother and the saints in heaven. In heaven, she reminded herself, time and space cease to exist, and she could freely visit the entire universe. There she could know God as he is and join the choir of angels in eternal praise.

———•——•——•———

Chic managed to take care of all the funeral arrangements. He made sure all the family was notified. He tried to relieve Suzy of all these earthly burdens so her full efforts could be directed to adjusting to her mother's murder.

The funeral service was well attended at the North Creek Baptist Church. All the politicians were there to be seen. The curiosity seekers were out in force. The preacher was short and to the point on the Gospel in the sermon and long on the family history.

Suzy was basically in a state of suspension and was unaware of what was going on around her until she was jolted back to the present as Chic sang "Amazing Grace" and "When Peace Like a River."

Chic sang like an angel, but perhaps more importantly, he was capable of wrapping his spirit around one's soul as he sang. Somehow, as he sang, one's soul would rise to a place of peace and comfort. What he might be unable to accomplish as a clinical psychologist, he accomplished through his spirit as expressed through song.

On the way back home, Suzy opened up to Chic about her decision.

"Chic, I've decided I'm not going to allow all the evil ones in the world to rule my life. If I allow myself to live in fear of death, or anything else in life, then it means my faith is weak. I believe that when Christ told us if we have faith of a mustard seed, we could move mountains, he was serious. I'm going to un-wad my panties and join you in the battle against evil."

"We'll do this together, Suzy. We are both going to need a full dose of positive energy to tackle these demons head-on."

Chapter

14

For Fort Walton Beach, Florida, it was a cold, rainy morning. Chic and Heath met for breakfast at Joe and Eddy's to review their next step in the case, based on the attack at Lake Izabal. After all the efforts they made, including Danny being shot and the other catastrophes following the investigation, it seemed that the only solid information they had was the name of the boat owner and corporation, known as Echeneis. Heath had checked the records, and there was a corporation by the name of Echeneis that was owned by a Belize corporation. The yacht, *Angel*, was registered in Panama.

"What kind of name is Echeneis?"

"Good question, Heath. Echeneis refers to a mythical creature that could stop or sink ships. In modern times, it refers to what we call a suckerfish. A suckerfish attaches itself to sharks and, I believe, to other large fish. I always think of them as having a symbiotic relationship with the shark. They hang onto the shark and live off the crumbs left from the shark's feeding.

"I have gotten all the public information I can find, which only reveals that Echeneis is a Belize corporation owned by another corporation. In other words, we will not find any real people we can identify by running down this daisy chain. However, having the name is helpful. We are checking to see if this company shows up anywhere in the chain of loans and other business dealings with the core list of corporations and companies I have identified. Eventually, we will identify companies on whom we can focus our attention.

"At some point, Chic, we will have to identify the culprits who have a nexus with the drugs and murders in our core case. We are getting closer to the organization behind Ken but not close enough to make any arrest. My intuition tells me we are closer than we think."

"I sure hope your intuition nails a real human soon. Our resources are limited."

"Here's the part that has to remain between us. Perhaps we can bring in Danny because we need some real undercover work here. Until I'm sure, I'll not tell Suzy or anyone else why I'm convinced we have a spy in the Renfro family."

"What do you mean we have a spy, Chic? I thought when Ken disappeared, our insider information problem was over."

"Here's the thing. Only you, me, Danny, Suzy, and the Renfro family knew that Danny and I were headed to Belize on a particular date. The Renfro family didn't know when we actually got to Fronteras because I didn't give them a specific time frame. It's clear to me that moving *Angel*, as well as the murder of Doug and Captain Hayes, and the attempt to kill me and Danny were all a response to my coming to Fronteras to continue my investigation. I'm certain that you, Suzy, Danny, and I didn't reveal any information about this case. If the source of the information came from any of us, that would require them to have a full-time tail on us. Had that happened, we would have some sign that would've tipped us off."

"That leaves someone in the Renfro family as our culprit."

"The murder of Suzy's mother, Margie, Captain Hayes and Doug, the attack on me, they all happened shortly after I talked to the Renfro family about my trip to Belize. The timing is so close that we have to conclude that the arrow points to somebody in the Renfro family. I think we need to send Jimmy Amos to Tennessee and let him check out each of the Renfros. My belief is that one of this family has recently come into some money that is being hidden from the rest of the family. So, we direct our attention to the money trail. We are dealing with a real live demon here."

"Sounds good to me, Chic. You get everything you can off the Internet, and we will find what we can recover from bank records of the Renfros. Then let's get together with Jimmy and see where he needs to direct his attention in Tennessee. If we find that one of the Renfros has come into some real money recently, we can bet that is our source of the leak."

"Now, I have also formed a conclusion about the case based on the name Echeneis. Actually the perp who named this company has a twisted sense of humor. It could also be a self-destructive impulse at work. Many times a criminal is caught simply because they need to brag or they need to flaunt their achievements. With any criminal endeavor of this size and scope, there are always too many moving parts to remain totally secret. What the name tells me is that the culprit is not the major corporation itself but is a group of employees who feed off the small crumbs of major financial deals of the parent company. For example, the bank could issue bonds secured by mortgages and sell the securities on the open market. Here, the culprits can anonymously buy a portion of the bonds. The group could also control some of the mortgages and other assets that the bank buys for use as security. These investments could be kept at a low level, making it difficult to detect."

"Do you mean, Chic, that the group we are after hides in the shadow of the large, legitimate bank or financial house, which may not have any official knowledge of the illegal activity?"

"Basically, yes. I think you can superimpose on the picture that the financial institution itself could be involved in larger schemes dealing with countries like Iran, North Korea, and Russia, who are dealing with getting around international sanctions or simply absconding or misdirecting the assets of the country. Size, scope, confusion, and greed all work together to provide cover for these operations. Since we now have a good handle on their business plan, we can more keenly focus our laser of truth in the right direction."

Chic and Heath worked out a basic plan of action. Heath called Jimmy and worked out the details as to the overall design of the plan to snoop on the Renfro family. Heath authorized the use of long-range recording devices as well as other snooping gear. Jimmy would be provided financial information as Chic and Heath uncovered that information.

Jimmy had reviewed all the material Chic and Heath provided him. Chic provided a written analysis of the Renfro family along with his thoughts of who among them was the most likely traitor. Chic had all but ruled out the mother and father as the possible traitor. His opinion was that it was an equal bet between the two children, Myra North and Dr. John Renfro. Sibling rivalry stood out as the primary motivator. Myra was the oldest by eighteen months. John appeared to be the more successful. He had more toys and appeared to be more socially adroit.

Myra was clearly inclined to be the bossy one, although not as bossy as her mother, Ann. On reflection, Chic had picked up a little tension between the siblings. Chic had the impression that Myra had a low level of resentment toward the younger brother. Nothing specific he could point to. Perhaps a shadow between them. Sometimes an older child resents the attention the parents give a younger sibling. There they were, the center of the parents' world, and along comes this brother or sister who steals their attention. John's relationship with the parents was more relaxed than Myra's.

Jimmy decided to start with Dr. John Renfro. It was easy to see that John was a lot less observant than Myra. Myra would actually present a challenge.

Jimmy scoped out John's house and office. Nothing out of the ordinary. He followed him to a mini storage unit that turned out to be half-empty. Jimmy attached a bug to John's car, which yielded nothing of interest. John's phone calls were monitored, but nothing unusual there either. Chic and Heath were able to check on the banking records of John, which appeared normal in every way. He had the assets one would expect of a successful doctor. He appeared to be an open book. Jimmy concluded that John was the kind of guy who was not capable of hiding substantial assets or anything else from his family members.

It became apparent early on that Myra was a complicated person. First, she was keenly aware of her surroundings. Nothing escaped her attention. Jimmy had to use all his training to escape her watchful eyes. He began to appreciate Chic's decision to use someone she didn't know for this job. He was thankful he was using a local car with a Tennessee tag. She would have picked up a Florida tag in a minute.

Jimmy scoped out her house and compared what he could see with Google images, satellite images, and building records from the city. Her house was on a large lot in a nice area. It appeared to be in line with what one might expect a college professor to own. The building records, however, showed a recent addition to the back of the house, which couldn't be seen from the road. He would have to actually go onto the property to see the kind of improvements that had been made.

Jimmy dressed as a building inspector and proceeded to investigate Myra's property. Thankfully, she didn't come home during this time. What he saw was a very nice addition—a two-car garage, plus living quarters above, consistent with the plans filed with the city. The quality of construction was first rate. He was able to see inside through glass panels in the garage door and could make out two Mercedes, worth well over $300,000. He couldn't determine exactly, but one was an S class sedan, and the other was two-seater sportster. Myra was a lady with secrets. The addition was at least two thousand square feet. The cost of the cars and addition would approach $800,000 or more. Myra didn't make that kind of money.

Jimmy added to his calculations that she was driving a very conservative Ford Taurus to work every day.

Myra's bank records showed a balance of $100,000. She also had a large safety deposit box.

Heath was able to obtain records showing Myra was scheduled to fly to Belize within a few days. The Belize connection was clearly a red flag.

Jimmy had managed to plant a bug in Myra's Taurus and a relay to amplify her telephone connections. With this equipment, he could pick up the number she was dialing. He was not tapping the phone lines or making any illegal intrusions onto her property.

Jimmy didn't have to wait long to get some results. On his first Friday night, he picked up a coded phone call to some guy. The call lasted thirty minutes. He was able to record the dial tone and frequency of each digit of the phone number. The problem was that the encrypted call was made through a relay system that effectively blocked their ability to trace the call. Why would an English professor be privy to any information that needed protection of this magnitude?

As Jimmy contemplated the implications of this information, he saw the Mercedes roadster come down the driveway and take a left turn toward downtown. The hardtop was down. He was able to get the tag number before she made a left turn. Jimmy called in the tag number for a full history of the vehicle. It was difficult, but he was able to stay just close enough to her to not get lost.

Ten minutes later, Jimmy pulled into the parking lot of a night spot where Myra was parked. This looked like a location that was frequented by the young and restless. Business was brisk. Jimmy watched a few guys go in, and he determined his outfit passed the dress code of the night. The action inside was brisk. It sort of reminded him of a bunch of peacocks in heat. Myra was standing at the bar, allowing some fancy dude to snuggle up way too close. She was dressed for action. She had on a tight red mini dress. The low-cut blouse exposed her ample breasts, with her hard nipples clearly exposed through the silk like material. Jimmy got the feeling that this girl was at home in chains and things. Myra was ready for action—she was the action. She allowed the boys to play, but she was in charge of the game.

Jimmy was struggling with himself. He had played this game before. He knew she was looking for just the right kind of guy to play some sick games with her tonight. He watched the amateurs buzzing around her, none with the right vibes. Jimmy decided to take a shortcut in his investigation. He slowly moved in for the kill. He nudged the guy sniffing her ear out of the way. He did so in the manner of the tough guy he once was.

He caught her eyes; the connection was instant.

There was some electrical impulse flowing between these two on an animal level. Before tonight, Jimmy had managed to calm the beast of his soul. Tonight was going to be a test. He never lost sight of the animal nature of humans, which would howl at the moon if left unchecked. The demon before him called, and he answered. His silent prayer was that he could harness the beast when the night was over.

She liked it when Jimmy pulled her roughly against his body. She felt his arms and purred about how strong he was. She pinched him with her long fingernails to test his reaction to pain. They embraced; she bit his neck. The experimentation continued for an hour or so while they drank, danced, punched, sucked on ears, and explored the possibilities for the night's activities. Jimmy was satisfied that this vixen was into pain, whips, and boots, but mainly she was looking for a subject who would freely play games with her.

Jimmy found himself in the passenger seat of the roadster as Myra drove like a bat out of hell through the streets of Nashville. Jimmy got focused on her exposed breasts and her shaved pant-less gates of hell. His brain was racing with anticipation, and he kept banging the dashboard and imploring her to get this piece of shit home.

The night was a blur. Jimmy was sure that in his younger days he might have experienced such a wipeout, but he didn't think so. He had enough bruises to convince him he had experienced some new ways to satisfy his sexual drive. Myra bore evidence of giving as well as receiving. He stood naked, facing this beautiful naked woman in black boots. His physical strength was totally nil. She, on the other hand, looked ready for more action.

Jimmy begged off and had to get on his knees to beg her to call a cab. While he was on his knees, he was required to provide a little more personal attention. He was shocked that after a night of heavy action, he still had enough left to find this demon mesmerizing. From some echo chamber in his head, he recalled saying, "Yes, yes, my love. I will join you and Larry in Belize."

Ten hours later, Jimmy awoke in his bed, fully clothed and feeling like shit. Now he remembered why he gave up the wild side of life. He lay there, trying to figure out how this woman had enticed him into behavior he had only read about in books. He had always been satisfied to get a piece of ass, roll over, and go to sleep. Most women were fairly happy with that kind of arrangement.

Myra was totally involved with masochism, bondage, and more ways to experience sexual pleasures than he knew existed. And what exactly did she have in mind for him and the guy name Larry? She had even volunteered to pay his way!

How am I going to make a full report to Heath and Chic? After a good deal of soul searching, Jimmy decided that total truth was necessary. He had no doubt that whatever the story was, Myra's sexual habits played a big part.

Jimmy requested the meeting take place somewhere other than Joe and Eddy's, somewhere private. Chic called the meeting at his office.

"Jimmy," said Chic, "I gather from your phone call that your meeting in Nashville was very exciting."

"Yes, I would say too exciting for me. Chic, you and Heath know I'm not exactly an angel. In the detective business, we don't get too many angels. Let me tell you that Myra is a devil in a woman's body. She had me sucked in like a baby. If she had asked me to jump out the nearest window to prove I could fly before she gave me another sexual encounter, I would have. After a night of whips, chains, pain, bondage, and sex in every position possible, she was still not satiated. She made me promise I would join her in Belize. There we would continue with the fun and games with her friend and benefactor, Larry."

Chic looked at Jimmy with his Cheshire cat smile. "What do we know about Larry?"

"Myra wouldn't tell me much about him, except that he is her lover. She referred to him as her business partner and led me to believe he provided her financial support. She told me he is a big banker in Boston. Beyond that, I concluded he must like chains and things. I can tell you this: to keep up with Myra, he must be some kind of stud horse. She let me know that Larry was her man. Me, well, I'm just some kind of play toy. She told me some of the things they like to do. Shocking! They both like to bring in other boys and girls.

"The question, guys, is do I have to go to Belize and take one for the team?"

Heath spoke up first. "One thing we know is that she and Larry are very dangerous. Do we know what their plan is if you do go to Belize? The odds are that you may not come back alive."

"I agree with that, Heath. Jimmy could be killed. He might also be warped for the rest of his life. I like undercover work, but we also have to be mindful of the price our agents pay. You can't have agents out shooting people just to prove themselves. You can't have agents like Jimmy taking a chance on warping his mind forever. It's not worth the risk."

"You're right about that, Chic. Jimmy has already convinced me that Myra is the one who profited from Ken's apparent death. We know she's hiding a substantial sum of money from her family. We know her friend's name is Larry and that he's a Boston banker. We know that Echeneis is located in Belize, where Larry and Myra want Jimmy to visit. If Jimmy goes to Belize, he can find out what Larry looks like, but that won't matter if he's dead."

"To be honest, Heath, if we send Jimmy to Belize, we might fill in a few more pieces to the puzzle, but perhaps there are other ways we can get the same information. I think we can assume that since Myra is the beneficiary of Ken's money, he's dead. Second, it follows that Larry had some connection to Ken's death since he was able to direct the money to Myra, who is Ken's sister. Third, I believe Larry is employed by one of the banks I have identified in Boston. Before we put Jimmy in danger, I'll see what I can learn about the bank Larry works with in Boston. Hopefully, we won't need to make that decision about sending Jimmy to Belize. However, we need to leave open this option. Myra likes Jimmy, and that gives us an opening if we need it."

As soon as the meeting concluded, Chic called Suzy with instructions to check Boston Capital World Bank Company (BCWB) for upper-echelon officers with the name Larry, probably between thirty and forty-five years of age. He then began to put in place plans to track Myra on her trip to Belize.

Chapter

—⁓ *15* ⁓—

Gilman Loeb (Sam) called a special meeting in his office at BCWB with David Richburg and Larry Moses, his partners in the banking end of the investment wing of Sinaloa cartel. Sam was the CEO of the international bank. David and Larry were officers of the bank and also were part of the executive committee. Sam liked the idea of being this close together.

"Gentlemen, first I want you to know that Max blew up Julius and most of the banking personnel of the Zeta gang, just as he said he would do. Problem is you have to assume that Zeta will come after us in some form of retaliation. So, David, make sure our security is tightened up."

"Yes, sir, you can all count on it. If you see anything out of the ordinary, call me immediately."

"The next problem is that our assassins killed Doug and Captain Hayes, but Chic managed to kill them."

"David, as promised, Chic is your trophy, unless you and Larry work out some other deal."

"David and I will have to discuss that. We'll work it out."

"As you guys know, my wife, Doll, has been carrying on an affair with Chic since college. Now, she and her friend Barbara have been placed in charge of the Alzheimer's telethon—and guess what? Chic is to be one of the featured singers. So he is going to be here in Boston, and Doll will actually be working with him."

"How many ways are they going to work together?" Larry said with a half grin on his face.

"Here's the thing," interjected Sam. "Whatever you think about Chic and your wife, you've got to play it clean until after the telethon. We can't be like the Mexicans and run off half-cocked. Look me in the eye, David, and tell me that you will hold off until after the telethon."

David finally grunted, "Okay."

———•———•———•———

Barbara and Doll arranged to meet at Doll's country club to work on the telethon. These ladies were great friends and running buddies. They knew each other's most cherished secrets.

"Barbara, I'm not exactly sure what David does for a living. I have a bad feeling that he's up to no good. I'm not sure what he would do if he found out about my friend. David could be really dangerous if he finds out."

"Look, Doll, David's not going to hurt you. He works with a large international bank as their security officer, so he comes in contact with some pretty bad characters. You've got to expect that strange information can get confused in his head, especially when he's drunk. So cool it. Give it some time and see what happens."

"Now we've got to get to work on the fundraiser in Boston and one in Atlanta for the Alzheimer Research Fund. I'm the chair for Boston, and you're the chair for Atlanta. I've worked up the committee members and the general outline of both events."

As Doll got into the details of the plans, she was able to temporarily forget about her problems. In fact, when she realized that Chic was going to be on the project in Atlanta, she actually let a smile creep across her face. Chic was a senior at Florida State when she was a freshman. He was a legend as the best tenor to ever come through Florida State, a school famous for its football and music. She wouldn't say that she had a crush on him, but there was something about this guy that she really trusted. Right then, having somebody to trust would be wonderful.

"Nancy, to be honest, David is convinced that Chic and I have been lovers since college. When he finds out that I will now be working with Chic, he may go truly nuts. Somehow, David has developed a special hate for Chic."

"Look, you can't let all that interfere in this telethon. Chic is a big guy, and he can handle David."

"Okay. I guess you're right."

The ladies finished their business and went their separate ways home. For some reason, Doll decided to take the long way home instead of taking the freeway. She was going through an upper-middle class community when she noticed a Baptist church with a flashing revival sign out front. The service was in progress. Doll was not a religious person. Her family rarely attended church. David was a reformed Jew, but he never attended service and was not a practicing Jew. She had attended a Baptist church in Tallahassee, Florida, a few times while in school. The first time, she went specifically to hear Chic Sparks perform. The man was unbelievably good. On another occasion, she attended a service as a fill-in violinist in a string quartet.

Doll found herself in the parking lot of the church as though some unseen hand had led her there.

She sat there for a short while, collecting her thoughts. She heard the choir singing from inside the church. At this distance, the sound was heavenly. Why was she here? Was this really happening? She wasn't the kind of person who easily gave in to her emotions. She rarely listened to her inner voice, but here she was, staring at the front door of a church. The next thing she knew, she was inside the church, and her burdens lifted from her heavy heart as her spirit soared in harmony with the congregation.

Doll's secret was just that—secret. Some things you don't repeat, even to your friends. She had to be careful with her husband, David. She was convinced he was a killer, but she knew she couldn't let him know about her fears. It was possible that she was wrong, that she herself could be the crazy one. She had faced this possibility many times, but when she calmed down, her logical mind told her she was mentally stable. If David heard the name Chic, he would go into a rage. If she tried to pray with him or speak to him about his soul, she could see the very devil rage in his eyes.

The Alzheimer's telethon was just forty-five days out, and she had worked through her problems. Part of her problem was she had to finalize plans with Chic, who was the featured artist at this event. The next forty-five days were central to the success of the fundraiser. She knew this would be dangerous for her and Chic. Doll was familiar enough with Chic's story to know that Suzy was the reason he had been sucked into investigating the Pensacola murders. God does speak in strange ways, she thought. Somehow it seemed preordained that she was going to draw Chic into her own problems with David. Did God have a unique plan to punish Chic by casting him into the lion's den with two damsels in distress?

Doll backed off her efforts to save David's soul and moved away from any form of confrontation. She began to make a journal listing everything she considered worthy of suspicion. She knew that when she talked to Chic, he would need this kind of information. She concluded that David was involved with Larry and the CEO, Gilman. She deduced that they had some business located in Belize. She was convinced that they had some connection with South American business, although she couldn't be specific. She couldn't be sure, but she felt like Boston Capital World Holdings Company was an enabler, though not directly involved in the criminal activity.

Doll knew the date of an upcoming board meeting of some kind that was going to be held in Belize in a couple of months. This was a topic of conversation among the families mainly because the females were not invited. She listened to the gossip from the wives, which reflected on the group's business operations in Belize. David noted that this was not going to be an official board meeting of the BCWB.

Doll checked and edited her journal until she was satisfied with the quality of her work. She was not specific enough to send anyone to jail with this information alone, but Chic could use her information to fill in blanks in his information. The total package should give her husband and his buddies terminal stomachaches.

Doll put the information on triplicate thumb drives that were hidden in a safe place. Her handwritten notes were burned. One of the thumb drives was sent to Chic in a box containing information about the telethon.

Doll and Barbara boarded a morning Delta flight to Atlanta, where they had a planning session with the performers, producers, symphony director, and other people in charge of the telethon. The event was to begin the following evening at 7:00 p.m. The music consisted of popular tunes and selections from Verdi's *Rigoletto*, *Aida*, and *La Boheme*.

Chic, along with the other singers, were all warming up for a few short runs along with a general walk-through of the program.

Doll and Barbara were going over the checklist with the producers and the team that would act as hosts of the event. It looked like a regular army setting up the phone lines as well as the area where volunteers would solicit donations. Doll was amazed that she and Barbara were able to pull off an event this large. Doll watched Chic run through his vocal exercises with what she could only describe as animal lust. Whatever the X factor was in human nature, Chic had it. She remembered pining over him from afar as a freshman at Florida State.

Doll was awaked from her dream by a vivacious and beautiful redhead who came straight up to her, looked her in the eyes, and said, "Hey, Mrs. Richburg. My name is Suzy. It's a real pleasure to meet you. I'm impressed with the job you ladies are doing."

"Suzy? Are you the Suzy who belongs to Chic?"

"Actually, we sort of belong to each other," Suzy responded with her usual big smile.

"Suzy, please call me Doll. I may not be one, but it helps my feelings when people call me Doll."

"Quit pulling my leg, Doll. All you have to do is watch the men around here watch you, and you know you're a knockout. I'm going to be sure to hold onto Chic when he comes over here to meet you when he finishes his warm-up. We want you to know we have gone through all the material you sent us, and we are duly impressed. Can we talk to you tomorrow morning?"

"Of course. I wouldn't miss that for the world. Suzy, I've followed all the stories in the paper about the many times you've avoided death, and I'm impressed. It's an honor to meet and get to know you."

Doll was really impressed by this young woman. She couldn't blame Chic for latching onto her. Somehow, the fact she really liked this girl made it easier for Doll to take her schoolgirl fascination with Chic out of her mind. Her mind needed to be unfettered when she did talk to Chic.

Chic finally finished and wandered over to Suzy's side. "Chic," said Suzy, "this is Doll and Barbara, the ladies who are in charge of this event."

Chic gave Doll and Barbara his best smile and shook both their hands. "Ladies, what a pleasure to meet you. You have done a wonderful job laying everything out in an orderly fashion. Let me tell you, I would walk from Pensacola to Atlanta to sing the *Rigoletto Quartet* number with this group. That's absolutely my favorite aria. In high school, we had a male quartet that had a parody of the *Rigoletto Quartet* number. It began with arguing over the correct way to pronounce Verdi and ended with pie in the face."

"Well, Chic," said Doll, "could we interest you in putting that stunt on tomorrow night?"

"I tell you what. This event is scheduled to go on until about 1:00 a.m. eastern time, isn't it?"

"Yes it is. What do you have in mind?"

"If I can talk my fellow artist into it, maybe around 12:30 a.m. we could do the special stunt for the folks in California. I won't make any promises. You know how actors can be, especially we opera types. Our britches can get so tight we can't even bend over."

"Let me know on that, Chic. We have plenty of time to work it in. We have built in enough flexibility to allow a few extra pieces if needed. As you know, the TV audience can request to hear a performer's best-known recording, which we'd like to do if we have the time."

"Doll, I understand you were at Florida State the same time I was there. Is that true?"

"Yes, that's true. I was a freshman, and you were a senior. I hope you don't mind my telling you that I had a young girl's crush on you. You know how silly young girls are. I actually had the opportunity to hear you perform several times. I was as impressed then as I am now. How is it that you became a clinical psychologist instead of a full-time performing singer?"

"Good question. I'm humbled that you had a crush on me. I hope I'm not too much of a disappointment in person. I have many reasons, of course, for becoming a psychologist, but when I direct my doctor self onto my inner self, I'm not sure I know the real reason. In a nutshell, I didn't believe I could make a steady living as a singer. It is too uncertain as a profession. Then I recognized I'm more comfortable around plumbers than I am around many musicians. I like the idea of being able to choose when and where I sing. While I make money with my recordings and with my appearances, my life's self-esteem does not depend on it. So I like the idea of singing purely for the love of singing, not out of necessity. In my quiet moments, this is what I tell myself."

"Chic, I'm not the psychologist here, but it sounds good to me. Suzy, I hope you don't mind my saying so, but we need to remember that Chic could sell me anything."

"I don't mind. Chic has the same effect on me. The great thing is that Chic is a straight shooter, and he will not lead you down a blind alley."

"Ladies, now cut it out. I'm prone to get a big head without the help of you beautiful women stroking my ego. I must admit that I do appreciate being stroked a little bit. We need to move on to the serious business at hand. Doll, when can we talk to you privately?"

"How about in the morning for breakfast here at the hotel?"

"Sounds good," said Suzy. "What time?"

"How about 7:00 a.m.? I've got a big day, so I need an early start."

"Suzy and I will be waiting on you at seven. Come by yourself. We don't need any extra ears."

Chic, Suzy, and Doll met at the hotel's restaurant at 7:00 a.m. sharp, but it proved difficult to find a private corner.

"Doll, Suzy and I can always find a private corner at the Waffle House. Have you ever eaten at a Waffle House?"

"I've heard about them, but you know it's a little under the circle I move in. If the ladies at the bank find out I'm eating in that kind of place, I would never live it down."

"Relax yourself. We are going to the Waffle House down the street where no one cares about listening to us. There is simply no privacy here."

As Chic and group moved toward the street, Chic picked up a tail. He was a dark-looking man about five feet ten, dressed in Boston clothes, which made him stand out to Chic. Chic could identify this guy as a killer, but he was no stalker. It was obvious to Chic that this guy hadn't taken into account that people in Boston don't dress like rednecks in the south. In fact, Chic picked the man out as soon as he turned to exit the hotel in an attempt to follow Chic's group. Chic was amused that the guy was trying too hard to look normal and appear as one of the many tourists. It was obvious to Chic that he and these ladies were being followed.

As Chic and group went into the Waffle House, he could sense the man knew he was in trouble if he actually followed them inside. The more the man tried to look inconspicuous, the more he stood out to Chic.

Chic kept the information to himself. No need to concern the ladies. Chic was confident that on the way back he would see the tail once again. Meantime, he was in a place he could talk. More importantly, he was packing. He had his .38 pistol in his pocket. It couldn't be seen.

They sat in the booth in the far corner next to the window.

"Chic, I've not eaten in a place like this since I left Florida State. Thanks for reminding me that eggs and bacon are basically the same anywhere you go. The only difference is how much you are willing to pay."

"Doll, I have to tell you that I prefer a place like this for breakfast to a fancy restaurant. The eggs go down a little easier, but mainly, the people in here are not so full of themselves."

"I can appreciate that. There was a time, Chic, when my life was going nowhere. I had every material thing a woman could hope for. My husband is a successful businessman and banker. He has power, wealth, and high standing in the community. I had everything but piece of mind and happiness. Finally, I was driving home one day, brooding over my uselessness to the world, when I passed a Baptist church. I heard the singing. I saw the revival sign. I had not been in church since I was a child. I have no idea what led me to stop and go inside, but I did. Suzy, I was greatly moved by your conversion. I may not have gone into that church if not for your example. I felt like if it helped you, it could surely help me.

"I'm here with you and Suzy for reasons I do not fully understand. I know you are after the gang that tried to kill Suzy. I believe my husband may in some way be connected to that gang of thugs. I know he is becoming a true demon. I've tried to save him, but he does not respond."

"Doll, do you understand that you are in danger? If you are right about your husband, then all of us sitting here are in danger. The information you have given me is very damaging to your husband and his partners. With this information, I can make money laundering charges on him stick. We are short on viable evidence of drug dealing and murder, but that information may become available. Money laundering charges will put them out of business for a long time. Of course, with money laundering, you always have the issue of tax fraud, which itself is serious."

"Help me understand, Chic, why David has become more violent and vindictive as I become more involved with the church. He can see that my life has changed. He can see that my soul is at peace. He knows I am more loving toward him, but all he does is rebel. So here I am with you trying to destroy the demon I see instead of being on my knees praying for David."

"The war between good and evil is never ending. Sin killed Jesus Christ, which brought us victory over the grave and salvation. He arose from the grave, which provides us salvation through grace. As we approach Christ, sin will fight us, using what we think are our strong points against us. We are led to see how much easier life would be if we only used our talents for our own personal gratification. We are sucked in toward what seems an easy road. In the end, that point of light we are following becomes the white-hot flame of death.

"Sooner or later, sin is when we turn from God to our own way, which in the end is death. David is on that journey."

"I know there are many who would call me nuts for destroying my family. I know David's group is responsible for destroying many lives. Many more will die if you and Suzy are not successful in stopping them.

"David thinks you and I were intimate in college. He firmly believes you and I are lovers now, and nothing I say will change his mind. At his first opportunity, he will kill you."

"He has tried to kill both me and Suzy. He did manage to kill Suzy's mother. As you said, we are all on his kill list. I regard his entire gang as a pack of killers. The battle is now at issue."

Suzy looked at Chic with her coy smile. "You are so dramatic, Chic. Don't worry, Doll. I'll be right behind you all the way."

"Thanks. You and Suzy know that if you need me, I will give you whatever help I can," Doll said with her great smile.

They finished an outstanding breakfast at Waffle House and headed back to the hotel, each with their own thoughts. Chic was, for the first time, certain he was on the right track with solid information. He noted that the tail was still there and still as obvious as ever. In a way, he was happy to know that everybody was aware that the game was on.

Slowly, his upcoming performance tonight came into focus. A smile appeared on his face, his spirit lifted, and the fog of battle cleared. Within a few steps, a new man walked in Chic's shoes. Chic silently thanked God for the power of music.

The nationally televised telethon that night raised several million dollars for Alzheimer's research. Everyone agreed the parody of *Rigoletto Quartet* number, performed at twelve thirty eastern standard time, was the hit of the show.

Doll and Barbara pulled Chic off to the side when the show was completed and gave him a big hug and kiss. His cheeks actually turned a little red. Even Suzy thought his blush was funny as well as cute.

"Chic," said Barbara, "let me thank you for proving to me that you opera singers are not all a bunch of stiff britches. Next time you sing, Doll and I will be in the front row, acting a little like school girls."

"Look, I'm just happy to know all of you society women up in Boston can actually let your hair down. Any time you need me to sing at one of your benefits, please call me."

Doll pulled Chic and Suzy to her, wrapping her arms around both, and whispered, "Pray for me. I'm praying that when we meet again, you shall have tamed the dragon."

David received the tail's report with keen interest. David knew that the report was delivered through the colored eyes of a warped mind. David made of the information what he would. What secrets did his wife tell his adversary? David was quite certain that Chic pulled his wife into his bed with Suzy, where they sucked her clean of all she knew about his business while enjoying her fleshy favors. David knew Suzy liked threesomes. That was all he could see when he saw the three together. David began to delight in the details of how he was going to make Chic suffer a slow and painful death. He was determined to have this pleasure.

As he sat there, his anger grew. Screw what he told Sam. His rage overcame his discipline. David left and checked on Chic's car, which was in the parking provided for the telethon. From the shadows, he could see

Chic getting in the car without Suzy. Perfect. Just a gun battle between the two of them.

David got in his car and waited for Chic to exit. It was late enough that traffic was no problem in downtown Atlanta.

Chic exited in the Mustang, actually enjoying the night air, relieved that the performances had gone so well and that he had avoided a confrontation with anyone. At that moment, Chic saw the lights of a car quickly approaching. Chic knew an angry driver when he saw one. The driver approached quickly on Chic's side of the car. Chic pulled out his .38. As the attacker drew even with Chic's window, he fired two shots. Chic observed that the weapon appeared to be a 9mm.

This was not Chic's first ballgame. When the attacker approached, Chic slammed on the brakes at the right moment. He held his fire. The two shots the attacker fired missed their mark.

The attacker made a decent brake turn and headed back toward Chic.

The attacker was in a Mercedes two-passenger convertible sports car and was vulnerable to Chic, who was heading directly at him. The attacker checked out and swerved just in time to avoid a collision.

Chic made an expert pivot and was now facing the attacker. At that exact point, he fired two shots, knocking out the attacker's windshield and scaring the hell out of the attacker. The attacker accelerated around a corner, giving him cover, and quickly disappeared in downtown Atlanta.

Chic couldn't identify the attacker and didn't have time to get a tag number. He did, however, have a couple of bullet holes in his Mustang. Chic called the police and made a full report. He reported this as a drive-by shooting and said that he was unable to get any identification other than the make of the car. With his credentials, the police made quick work of this report.

The hard part, however, was telling Suzy, who rightfully would freak out.

Chapter

16

Chic and Suzy left Atlanta the next day after a very successful telethon. Chic didn't alarm Suzy by telling her of the gun fight. He had decided it was too much. He blamed the bullet holes in the Mustang on a drive-by shooting. The six-hour drive from Atlanta to Pensacola, Florida, gave them plenty of time to review their progress in this case. They took a couple of extra hours in Columbus, Georgia, for Chic to visit the Infantry Museum at Fort Benning, Georgia. This is a state-of-the-art museum dedicated to the history of Fort Benning and the men in the infantry. They left the museum with a deeper appreciation for the heroes who have given their lives in the service of this country. If Chic could have his way, every school child in the country would be required to visit that museum.

A short visit to the Schwob School of Music located at the River Center in downtown Columbus, Georgia, reminded Chic of the uniqueness of this venue as a mecca for the preforming artist.

A dinner stop for fish at Hunt's in Dothan, Alabama, rounded off what Chic should have been able to rate as the most fulfilling interlude in his life. With the murder of Suzy's mother, it was not to be. They both were facing severe frustrations. Suzy's anger was still overwhelming. Chic's training and experience as a clinical psychologist proved inadequate. There was too much personal conflict to allow him to see things from a professional viewpoint. Did he bear some responsibility for Margie's death? Had he called Suzy from Belize, would she have been able to warn her mother? This had crossed his mind, but he had concluded that Suzy would have been the target. He was beginning to believe that he had made a mistake in not at least letting Suzy know that he had been attacked in Lake Izabal.

As they drove down the road in silence, Chic began to believe that he was in shock. He had never expected to be affected like this. On the good side, Chic had the name and location of Ken's bosses in Boston. He could identify the cartel's business by name, knew their location, and knew how they operated, all of which was going to give him a shot at the bosses themselves. This one thought gave him some hope that he would be able to forestall another attack on himself and Suzy. This possibility was far too tenuous, and Suzy was far too shaky to give her any kind of false hope.

Chic knew from history that simply identifying a criminal, while essential, is only part of the job. Being able to nail them with specific crimes would be good, but this group of criminals would have to be eliminated for him and Suzy to feel safe.

Chic was totally out of sorts that he had to run from a gun battle in Atlanta without being able to identify the villain, and that he had to fight for his life in Lake Izabal. Suzy looked over and with a troubled look in her eyes asked Chic, "Why didn't you call me from Belize and let me know your life had been threatened? Maybe I could have warned Mother. What were you thinking? I needed to know you were hurt. I know that I'm in the middle of this, and I can't just wish away the threat in our lives. But I'm having a difficult time dealing with my mother's death and feeling like I'm helpful to you."

Suzy slid away from Chic as she drifted into a somber, defensive posture.

Chic clearly understood this stance. Perhaps it would be totally unnatural had she not responded that way. His prayer was that this situation would not put a wall between them.

"I have to confess, Suzy, that your mother's death is a low blow to you. I'm sure it was intended to pierce your heart, which it did. At the same time, it was meant to pierce my heart, which it did. It's my fault that I didn't foresee this attack in Lake Izabal. I didn't conceive that someone in the Renfro family would warn Ken's gang that I was on the way to Belize and Lake Izabal. That gun battle left me in a state of shock.

"Now I have to confess there was another attempt on my life tonight. I wasn't going to tell you for fear that it would push you off the edge. Frankly,

I'm still not sure I should have put this in your lap at this time. In truth, I plain need you. Whatever burden I have is not comparable to all that you have been through. So, while I need you, I hope that I can manage to help you bear the burden you are bearing."

"That's very kind of you, Chic. You will need to give me time to deal with my soul. In my heart, we must be able to trust and rely upon each other if we are going to survive this ordeal."

Chic took her hand. She slid back over to his side. He placed his arm around her shoulders and pulled her close.

"Here's the problem, love. We have a cartel composed of men who are the best at what they do. The Boston group handles the money manipulation. The cartel does the dirty and wet work. The Mexican cartel controls the drug operations. Until I see them all together in Belize, we can't really identify the cartel principals. Then we really don't have a handle on their banking operations in Belize. But mainly, if we don't put this crowd out of operation, our chances of surviving this are nil."

"How can you ever run this to ground?" asked Suzy.

"That's our problem. We're only partway there. That's one reason I need to lay my eyes on these people, quickly. It's our only chance."

"I see your point, Chic. In a strange sort of way, the only person on our radar who has a relationship with the gang is Myra. Perhaps she, more than Doll, is actually the wormhole into the heart of the demon. Doll knows a lot about David, but only Myra knows anything about their activities and schedule."

Heath and Chic met the next day. Chic gave a detailed report on the information he had gathered along with his plan to go to Belize to see what he could find.

"Heath, the cartel in Boston don't have a joint meeting like this one in Belize but a couple of times a year. I really need to visually identify the Mexicans and the Boston group. Then we have Myra going down at the same time. She obviously has a close relationship with the Boston group. We've seen the cartel's tracks, but this time I need to actually see the real actors. Heath, I can't let this opportunity pass. Mine and Suzy's lives depend on it. I've got to take them out."

"Chic, I hate to agree with you on this. You're going to be exposed as hell, but you know the risks."

"Well, Heath, today is my time. My intuition tells me that I don't want to miss the action I'll see on this trip.

"Heath, the one logistical problem I have is actually finding Myra and Larry when I get to Cancun and then keeping them under surveillance. I'm going to need some help to pull that off."

"Well, you're in luck. Danny has a cousin in Belize who operates a fishing boat in Quintana Roo. I believe his name is Juan. Do you want me to line him up for you?" Arrangements were made to meet Juan in Belize City. Juan was to provide the boat.

The gunfight in Atlanta had convinced Chic that at this point there was no hiding. They would be watching him as he watched them. They would be waiting for the first opportunity to take him out.

Chapter

17

Myra was tooling down a back mountain road outside of Nashville like a bat out of hell in her two-door Mercedes handmade sportster, top down, red scarf flying, experiencing the adrenalin rush she so craved. Springtime in the mountains. All nature was springing into growth after a hard winter. The sap was on the move in the trees in the miracle that brings new life every year. She could feel her own juices flowing as she envisioned the many pleasures she would experience with her lover, Larry, at the upcoming meeting in Belize.

How blessed was she to be brought into the confidence of these bankers from Boston and Mexico. No wives were allowed. Only she would actually meet the group in their sanctuary. She knew she fit into their plans and would perform any task assigned to her. Her contact with the Russians would be extremely important.

Teaching a bunch of young pricks in college was useless. It was not exciting. What did it accomplish? The students had no real interest in literature. Where was the meaning? Well, on the good side, she decided that teaching gave her cover as a respectable citizen. People would never guess that she had a small part to play in a worldwide business venture. When you have power over the life and death of people, you approach a peak that elevates you above the crowd. Above the unnecessary people, the pissants you can stomp out at will. She was being called to the high place of power. She deserved it. She wouldn't disappoint.

The grand day of the meeting in Belize was at hand. All of the parties had made their separate plans to arrive at the company resort on their privately owned cay off Belize.

Larry and Myra arranged to meet in Cancun where they would then drive to an elegant resort in Tulum. They met there yearly to carry out a task that could hardly be described as joyous. They first went to the hotel in Tulum, dropped off their bags, and Myra went to the veranda, waiting on Larry. Myra remained quiet on the veranda, her mind drifting back to her days in Oxford five years earlier. She'd been in England doing the final research on her thesis, and she'd also come to give birth to Sissy. For five years now, her daughter was a secret to everyone in the world, except for Larry and the little girl's nanny.

Larry and Myra talked little on the way back to Tulum. Neither would qualify as a fit parent. Myra was satisfied that Sissy was in good hands in the home of Carla. Carla was able to provide a proper home for Sissy.

"Larry, you know I can't decide if I need to keep up this visitation or not. I know I'm not the motherly type, but I have to confess that these visits have an effect on me. I can't get into a partying mood until after we complete the visit."

"I'm sort of the same way, Myra. This little girl is beautiful, well behaved, and very smart. Carla does a wonderful job with her."

"She looks at Carla as her mother. You and I are simply her aunt and uncle. I really don't believe she remembers us from year to year. What do you think? Do we need to keep doing this?"

"At this point, I'll say we need to keep up this visitation. I'll make sure she is financially well off. At some point, though, I imagine we will just need to fade into the background."

"You know, Larry, it's not easy to say this, but your subconscious will hound you forever. I guess we will know when it is no longer in Sissy's interest for us to make these yearly visits. Even now, she's getting to the age when children don't really like to spend time with two strangers, as you and I surely are. Larry, your children are with you at home, so they fill your need for family. But when you go home to your family, no matter how hard I try, I do at times get lonely. I fight it, but at times I envision myself with a family. I know that's not realistic, but there you are. You can't hide from dreams."

Myra knew early in life she was different. Even at age nine and ten, she began to have a sexual appetite. She and her brother, Ken, were close, so he became her first target. They both lacked respect for authority and seemed to feel no guilt in their youthful experimentation. Myra was much smarter than Ken. She knew this and became their leader. Myra was confident and self-sufficient. She was a leader, pushy and smart enough to assert herself in any situation. Handling men was never a problem for her.

Carla was waiting when Larry and Myra arrived. Sissy and two of her friends stood at Carla's side, waiting for the two visitors. Myra gave Sissy a few presents, which she opened with delight. The kids were loaded into the car and taken to get ice cream. After a couple of hours, the kids ventured off to play on their own. They had had all the fun with adults possible.

The adults retreated to the veranda where they could watch the kids playing. Larry was sitting in a big wicker chair, nursing his drink, looking more like a college kid than the powerful executive he actually was. His ability to handle the financial affairs of the syndicate was unique. He had the ability to keep the intricate corporate structure in his mind. He did not have to refer to notes to move money around in a complicated dance that few could follow.

"Tell me, Carla, are you satisfied with our arrangement?"

"Yes, sir, Mr. Larry. You take very good care of me and my family."

"Are you having any problems with Sissy that we need to know about?"

"No, sir. She is a great kid. There is no question in her mind about me being her mother. She really doesn't remember who you are until I explain that to her when you come here. She really has no questions."

"Carla, let me give you this phone. It is only good for today and tomorrow. If you need anything during that time, please call me. We will be sure to take care of any problem before we leave."

The kids were called in, and they all had a snack consisting of candy, cake, and other goodies designed to please any kid.

Good-byes were said by all, and within four hours of arriving, Larry and Myra were on their way back to Tulum where they would spend the night at their exclusive resort. Myra, in the lizard part of her brain, however, still clung to a distant thought about her responsibility as a mother. The true miracle of motherhood, however, was becoming more and more distant even in the lizard part of her brain.

———•———•———•———

Chairman of the board of BCWB and number one of the triad sat at the head of the empty table reviewing his notes. Gilman had a round, friendly face with a permanent smile that could disarm his worst enemy. He would first meet with Larry and David to review the scheduled stockholders' meeting for the next day, followed by the grand reception where everybody who was anybody in Massachusetts would be.

Gilman found it somewhat amusing that in order for the triad to operate as they did, they had to be gifted magicians. Key to the deception was the large, legitimate bank BCWB, which had to be the center of attention at all times. It was the flashing object on which the public focused, allowing the sleight of hand, which was the criminal enterprise.

Gilman liked to refer to this group as the Echeneis, or suckerfish, to remind them that they fed off their host but never enough to kill or harm the host. The flashier the host became, the easier it was to conduct their business in darkness. The suckerfish had to remain small in relation to its host.

There were many elements about this charade that Gilman truly loved, but he was unable to identify a primary element. He loved the danger and the adrenaline rush it produced. He liked the nontaxed riches he was accumulating. He loved the power. As chairman of the board, he was powerful, but nothing was as powerful as the control over life and death. In the end, perhaps it was the fine art of deception itself that seemed to thrill him the most. What a stage on which to perform his magic.

Larry and David came in, and the three went over the business items that would be covered in the board meeting and the stockholders' meeting.

There was no reference to Belize at all. The tradition was to take a short vacation after the gala event each year. It was usually billed as a working vacation. As soon as the grand gala was over, the men would go to the airport where they would each depart to one of the major markets, Miami, New Orleans, or Houston, each in his private jet. From that point, they made their own private arrangements that would eventually land them in Belize.

Gilman had to acknowledge that even in this offline and secret activity, some planning was required, which would make it impossible for anyone to retrace their movements. No human activity can be done in a vacuum, which makes the sleight of hand more critical.

It is the nature of the human condition that people see what they want to see and hear what they want to hear. Most people are basically good and tend to trust people they know. They want to believe the best in the people they meet. All these natural tendencies become tools in the magician's toolbox. Gilman's toolbox was full. On top of that, he was a true, quintessential sociopath. He was the kind of guy who could cheat you over and over, and you would still trust him with your money.

Gilman was the chairman and number one because he was loved, even by those who knew he couldn't be trusted. Larry Moses and David Richburg served on the executive committee with him.

The full board of directors showed up for the regular monthly meeting. Chairman Loeb, as was his custom, conducted the meeting in an orderly fashion. There were no major issues to come before the board.

Following an uneventful stockholders' meeting the next day, a group of six hundred invited guests gathered in the grand ballroom at the home office building of BCWB for what was always billed as the event of the year in Boston. By any measure, the event matched its billing.

BCWB gathered national attention by donating $50 million for genetic research at the Harvard Medical School. There were at least twenty senators at the gala. Former president George Bush was there. The Bush family had already made secret donations to the medical school, but they did make the public event when he donated several of his paintings. There were enough generals and admirals to start World War III. The Kennedy family was there. It was rumored that their donation was in the neighborhood of $10 million.

The guest speaker was former president Bill Clinton, who also made the special presentation to Chairman Loeb in recognition of the $50 million donation to the Harvard Medical School. BCWB was the largest donor to Harvard in each of the last ten years. Chairman Loeb was totally humbled by the generous gesture from President Clinton, whom Chairman Loeb recognized as a fellow traveler in the universe of magic. After watching President Clinton, Gilman did not want to compare wand sizes with him.

Gilman totally amazed himself that his tear of humility was bona fide.

As the night wore on, BCWB began to develop a halo. Even the good works of Mother Teresa couldn't hold up to the bank's lofty level of goodness. Gilman had the distinct feeling that in the mind of this auspicious crowd, he had moved into the role of sainthood. His moon-shaped face, calm demeanor, and saintly smile seemed to predestine Gilman for this role.

———•———

Carmen, Gilman's girlfriend, was standing next to Gilman's wife, Judith, both of whom acknowledged that Gilman fit the part well.

"Well, Judith, your husband seems to have morphed into sainthood tonight. How does it feel to be married to Mr. Clean?"

"Good question, Carmen. Do you think we could wipe that smile off of his face if we told him you and I have a thing going on behind his back?"

Carmen gave that question a little thought, then answered, "You know, Judith, I don't know what he would do in private, but in public he wouldn't even blink. He would continue to smile as though he had just been told he won the lottery."

"I've often wondered about what he would do if he knew, Judith. What do you think?"

"You first, Carmen. You know the girlfriend always has the answers."

"Well, look at it this way, Judith. Girls have sex in a different way with each other than with boys."

"You're right. Go ahead."

"When you put a man in the middle, girls like us are in hog heaven, for the most part. Sometimes, of course, some resentment slips in. To boil it down, Judith, I think you and I might enjoy sex in a threesome with a lot of different men if they could handle it. But I believe Gilman would be nasty and would blow his gasket. His ego is far too big. So if he finds out, one or both of us would be seriously punished."

"That's a very good analysis of Gilman, Carmen. So, it seems you and I need to keep our little secret to ourselves."

"That's a good deal," said Judith. "Let's go to the powder room and kiss on the deal."

"Lead the way."

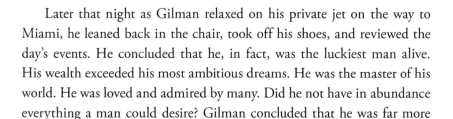

Later that night as Gilman relaxed on his private jet on the way to Miami, he leaned back in the chair, took off his shoes, and reviewed the day's events. He concluded that he, in fact, was the luckiest man alive. His wealth exceeded his most ambitious dreams. He was the master of his world. He was loved and admired by many. Did he not have in abundance everything a man could desire? Gilman concluded that he was far more powerful and important than anyone at the gala tonight realized. They would never know how humble he really was.

As Larry and Myra's car disappeared in the distance, Carla used her regular cell phone to call her cousin, Nicolas. Nicolas had explained to her that he was in charge of Larry's safety until he got to the private cay in Belize. She confirmed to Nicolas that they had just left and that they were going to Belize in the morning. She gave him their location in Tulum. Nicolas thanked her profusely for her part in assuring the safety of her boss, Larry.

Peppi, Jorge, and Hernandez were all sitting around a conference table in Hernandez's elaborate office, waiting on confirmation that Larry was present and that the meeting was on for the next day. Hernandez's office had a nice water view. The chairs were quality leather. The conference table was handmade. The phone rang and was answered by Jorge. "Nicholas, is that you?"

"Of course, Jorge. I'm calling to let you know Larry has left here and is headed to Belize."

"You are positive it is him?"

"Of course, Jorge. Let me know if you need anything else."

"Jorge, are we now ready to execute our plan?" asked Hernandez.

"Yes, sir. Everything is in place. Our operatives believe Larry and crowd are scheduled to meet at the resort first, and then we expect them to proceed to the yacht where the Boston group and the Sinaloa gang will conduct their conference. We've had to rely on several sources, but we are confident we are right. We, of course, know who runs the Sinaloa group. We've been able to track Miguel and will confirm when he actually boards the helicopter for this cay. We know they are all on the move, and by history, that means they are headed for their annual conference. The only one of the Boston group we have been able to pin down is the one known as Larry, as you heard from Nicholas. We are lucky that Nicolas discovered that his cousin is the titular mother of a child fathered by the banker from Boston."

"Okay, Jorge, I know you are good, but how in the hell did you find out that the Boston banker has anything to do with Sinaloa?" asked Hernandez.

"As much as I would like to think that this information came to me because of my brilliance, the truth is it was pure blind luck. Nicolas has been one of my operatives in Quintana Roo and Belize for many years. His family is from that area. When we need something in that area, he is our go-to man. He was able to place one of his cousins on the Sinaloa's private cay as a gardener. All he does is dig ditches, plant flowers, and do general hard labor. He has been there for over a year now. He can tell from the level of activity when some important event is going to happen. Based on his observations, the yacht is being provisioned for a big meeting, and the resort itself is under intense preparation for an important affair. The rumor is that the big boys are coming in tomorrow.

"Okay. This is the deal. Larry is like the point man in charge of the resort itself. He also seems to be the point man in charge of the business named Echeneis. This is the rumor at the resort. The rumor is that when he comes down here, he sometimes stops off at Tulum to see family members, so that is how we were actually able to put this together."

Hernandez came to a final conclusion. "Men, we're going to have to assume that the big guys are going to show up tomorrow in Belize and will be on the yacht."

Hernandez issued the order. "Get the men in place and make sure the divers are ready. Move."

Chapter

18

Myra was lost in her private thoughts as she returned to the resort near Tulum. Confronting her only child always left her in a confused and funky state of mind. She struggled with her inability to relate to her child. She could sense Sissy's ambivalence toward her. Myra's own narcissism left her no room for thoughts about how this might affect her only child in the long run. Myra couldn't help her thoughts going back to her own childhood. Her mother and father were wonderful toward her. How did she come to this place in her life?

Myra looked at her situation with Sissy as a disinterested scholar, analyzing the problem from a literary point of view. Myra could see that Larry, being a typical man, was satisfied that he was preforming his fatherly duties by supplying financial support as well as a substitute family that could provide all other needs the child might have. Analytically speaking, Myra knew one couldn't really delegate parental responsibilities.

Myra's mood turned dark. She hated Sissy's intrusion into her peaceful state of mind. Myra was certain Larry could bring a smile back to her face when they got home.

Myra didn't really understand why she had fallen into this funky mood. Despite her best efforts, seeing her child aggravated her soul in unexpected ways. By the time they arrived at their resort, she had concluded that their visits would have to stop. She knew that her motherly instincts barely existed. She had no desire to be a mother, so why in hell was she conflicted about this child? She didn't have time for this.

By the time they entered their marvelous bedroom, Myra was receptive to Larry's advances. For the moment, she was pleased to receive the attention and submit passively to his advances rather than being the aggressor. Larry stroked her gently. He kissed her in all the right places. Their spirits unified, morphing into sex on the gentle side. The exciting stuff would come later that night. Larry could read her moods before she was fully aware of them herself. They were, and had been from college days, true soul mates. The devil himself had to be pleased that two of his most dedicated disciples could make such discordant music in concert together. Truly a unique art form.

The light that led them down the wide road of sexual pleasure would eventually devour them. The white-hot breath of evil spares no one who gets too close to its light source.

They lay in bed satisfied. Myra had the vision of two turtle doves, cooing to signify their complete satisfaction. Crap—if she could sing, she would probably muster a cooing sound herself.

"Get your towel, Larry, and let's go lie on the beach in the nude."

"You got it, love. I want to brag on my honey anyway."

"Now, lover, I don't want to drag any extras into the bedroom tonight. Tonight, I'm going to be all the woman you can handle. I've got a few new tricks for you."

"I can't wait. We'll just go stir the pot on the beach. I'm sure I'll get excited when I tell you my plans for Chic. I might have to fight off some of those old whores who hang around the beach. All they do is drink their whiskey and watch the beach boys to see if any of them can actually drag their dong in the water."

Larry phoned the bar to have drinks ready at their cabana on the beach.

The sun was low on the western horizon. There was an onshore breeze. The beach was one of the most beautiful in the world. Off to the south, a group of nude teenagers in the prime of their lives were playing volleyball. Here, hedonism was in full bloom.

"My god, what a scene," muttered Larry.

"Why in the hell do we cover up the beautiful human body like we do, Larry? At least on a warm day like today, everyone should be required to go naked."

"Myra, if the people in the world all looked as good as the people on this beach, I would agree. But the fat, old farts with boobs hanging down to their knees should cover up."

"We'll solve that problem, love. We'll just hang around this kind of beach, where all the bodies are beautiful. Now, tell me your plans for Mr. Chic."

"I'll tell you this: before this time tomorrow night, Chic will be a dead asshole. I'm going to personally kill his ass."

"I thought the Mexicans handled all the wet work. Are you sure David will go along with this?"

"Yes, he will. We've discussed it and decided that the job is mine. The Mexicans had their chance and failed. David had his chance and failed. Now the job is mine. We have him under surveillance, and tomorrow it will happen."

"Well, I thought David had a grudge against Chic because he thinks Chic is screwing his wife. He believes they've been lovers since college."

"David and I talked about that. We both agree that I'm more physically fit and should be able to better handle Chic. I'm the one who has the physical strength necessary. Dave is a tough guy, but I'm bigger and faster than he. My training in the martial arts is excellent. Chic's a real badass, but I'm the man for the job. Then, I have the personal motivation to get even for you. Ken would still be around if Chic hadn't gotten in the way. I feel like I owe this one to you."

"That's awfully sweet of you, Larry. Ken was my brother. He and I were of a kindred mind. As kids, we used to talk about how we must have been adopted. Our mother, father, and brother have so much starch in their britches that they can't move freely and certainly cannot think out of the box. Ken and I kept our true lives secret from them. Of course, you know this."

"I know that you and he collaborated closely on his business plans for the company. I'm not so sure, but you actually originated most of his ideas. Is that true?"

"Yes, it is. I'm sure you know that I've never tried to insert myself into the affairs of the company, other than assisting Ken."

"We know that. That's the reason you're here. You're here because I want you here, but tomorrow you will be at the resort by the invitation of the company. They, or we, have some long-range plans that may need your talents. The group is particularly interested, as I have told you, in your connections with the Russians."

"Wonderful. I'm happy you guys trust me. I'm at your command when you need me. What exactly is going to happen tomorrow?"

"Basically, you and I will fly from here by private plane to the resort in Belize. I'll drop you off at the resort and take a helicopter back to Belize City. When I'm finished with Chic, I'll meet you back on the yacht."

Like teenage lovers, they stayed on the beach for the rest of the afternoon, watching all the lovely bodies strut their stuff up and down the beach. As the sun dropped below the horizon, they retreated to their room with just enough of a buzz on to kill any remaining inhibitions. The young naked bodies on the beach had been like war drums slowly mesmerizing them into a fevered pitch.

Their lovemaking this time was not a gentle caress. It was an attack of two animals drawing from each other the maximum amount of physical pleasure possible, along with a little pain. This kind of pleasure that, in the mind of the deviate, can only be fulfilled with pain and bondage.

Their sexual debauchery finally exhausted every ounce of energy in their bodies. They eventually collapsed as two spent ragdolls onto the bed, not moving until awakened by Larry's assistant banging on the door.

"Time to rumble," he said.

Larry acted as normal as possible as he and Myra boarded the twin prop plane at the private airfield near Tulum. His operatives kept him appraised of Chic's location through his earpiece. They were working under the delusion that Chic didn't know he was being followed.

Chic was sitting in a trashy-looking pickup truck, parked in the shade of a tree but not hidden. Chic was quite certain that he was being watched. He intended to be seen but to not be too obvious about it. He was dressed in what he considered local attire—white T-shirt, blue jeans, boots, beat-up cowboy hat, and day-old beard. His blond hair and light complexion clearly marked him as an American dressed as a Mexican. Chic knew there would be no confrontation here. He assumed it would be in Belize, where the cartel had substantial clout.

Chic got on his own private charter plane to take him to Belize City airport. He scheduled his departure to coincide with the departure of Larry and Myra from Tulum. His plan was to monitor the cartel group from Juan's fishing boat. Chic had the equipment delivered directly to Juan's boat, which was docked at a downtown fisherman's wharf. Chic arrived at the airport and was promptly taken to his rental car. Time was tight, but he should be able to get himself in position to monitor the cartel's yacht as it left the resort.

As Chic was flying over Belize, he marveled at the beautiful beach and the azure water of the Caribbean. It was hard to accept the magnitude of the evil he was dealing with. He knew he was out on a limb. If the cartel handled everything as they should, all he was going to see was a beautiful yacht day sailing off the coast of Belize.

On the good side, Chic knew the cartel was nervous. His presence had to make them look over their shoulder. They would worry about all the things they didn't know. They had to assume that Chic had backup. Had he been able to penetrate their resort with listening devices? Had he been able to place spies at the resort? Chic was hoping they had an active imagination. His big concern was that the cartel had many assets they could call upon to cause him personal harm. They could attack him from anywhere.

This was Chic's kind of game. Two adversaries in a nose-to-nose confrontation where neither could truly predict the hand of fate. Chic, a man of faith, had a simple belief that right would prevail.

━━━━━●━━━━━

Juan had his fishing boat docked near the San Pedro Ferry at the conjunction of the Belize River in the Caribbean. Juan was an averaged-sized Mexican. He had spent the morning cleaning the boat and making sure everything was ready for Chic. They had never met each other, but Danny had texted him a photograph of Chic over his iPhone. Juan was sitting in the captain's chair when he heard his name called out.

"Good to see you, Juan. How have you been?"

Juan looked at the man carefully, but the guy's face didn't register with him.

"Yeah, yeah," said Juan. "I'm having a hard time remembering your name and recognizing your face. Have we met?"

"Hell, Juan, I thought you would remember me. My name is Georgie. We met in Fronteras a few years back. I'm a good friend of your cousin, Danny."

"I guess I'm getting old. I can't remember that, but if you are a friend of Danny, come on board."

"Thanks, I appreciate that," said Georgie.

Georgie stepped aboard, and as he did, Juan turned to his left to get back in the captain's chair. As quick as lightning, Georgie rammed an ice pick into Juan's temple, jamming it into his brain. Juan fell onto his face, dead. No noise and very little blood.

Larry, who was standing close by, casually stepped into the boat. "Good job, Georgie. Let's drag Juan into the cabin. We'll place him in a storage bin underneath the bunk."

"Now remember, Georgie, you're playing the part of Juan. You have enough of his history to play the part. Chic has never met Juan, so you shouldn't have a problem. When he gets here, we'll have to move quickly.

"Put on Juan's hat and pull it down as low on your face as possible. Make yourself busy. You've worked on boats enough to make that look normal. I'll start the engine. We want to be ready to pull out as soon as Chic arrives. I'll be hiding in the cabin. Follow our plan on getting him to turn his back to the cabin so I can attack him from behind."

"I'll do my best," said Georgie.

"Now, if anything goes wrong, Georgie, you jump in and help take out Chic. I think I can handle this songbird myself, but if I need somebody, be ready."

Larry was deep in his thoughts about the exact method he would use to kill Chic. He knew the cartel guys looked upon him as a softy. They figured he was an educated fool who couldn't fight his way out of a paper bag. Larry prided himself, however, as a physical specimen. He ate only the right foods, stayed in fighting shape at all times, and considered himself basically superior to most other humans, including Chic. He knew he was a good athlete. In a way, he figured he had been training for a showdown like this all of his life. To move into the undisputed leader role of this unholy joinder of a drug cartel with a legitimate group of bankers required the spilling of blood—Chic's blood. As he waited for Chic to arrive, he carefully rehearsed every move he intended to make. Larry was confident his plan was unstoppable.

Chic's car, an old Ford Explorer, was waiting for him at the airport in Belize. He didn't waste any time hitting the road for Belize City. Danny had given him an old photograph of Juan, but the quality was so bad that the photograph was useless. Danny had given him a good description of Juan. Chic was confident that Juan would have everything ready to go.

Chic was cavalier and lighthearted as he hastened to the waiting boat. One way or the other, he was going to identify his enemies. Then he was going to find a way to eliminate them. They had made Suzy's life hell long enough.

Chic was delayed by a traffic accident for fifteen to twenty minutes getting to the boat, *Mermaid II*. Chic found himself more fidgety than normal. Then he got an uneasy feeling. Chic believed in his premonitions. His belief in them had saved his life many times. When he finally got out of the traffic jam, he forced himself to not drive too fast. He didn't need to be stopped by the police. There was no clock going. As soon as he spotted the boat, even before he spotted Juan, he had a sudden flash of danger. Juan had not seen him yet, so he took a little extra time sitting in his car trying to spot the source of danger.

Everything looked normal. The boat looked ready to go. *Mermaid II* looked like a perfect platform for this kind of caper. It was a typical thirty-foot fishing boat, locally made. It fit in with every other boat around and should look perfectly normal fishing near the cartel's island as well as coming close to the cartel's yacht. Chic carefully observed Juan, who was busy making sure everything was straight and that the equipment was laid out for easy access. Chic didn't notice any suspicious-looking men nearby. He saw no one other than Juan on the boat.

Chic fumbled with his gear in his car trunk, carefully analyzing every move of Juan. Okay, he didn't know Juan. This person he was looking at didn't really match Danny's description of his cousin. Finally, Chic focused on Juan's shoes. Juan had on street shoes made of excellent leather. Danny's cousin Juan couldn't afford that kind of shoe. No local fisherman would wear a street shoe on a boat.

Meanwhile, Larry was hiding in the cabin ready for his attack. He had received a message over forty minutes ago that Chic was on his way. He should have been there at least thirty minutes ago. He was getting hot and nervous. Larry didn't know if he was coming with help, so he felt like he could not reveal himself in the cabin.

Chic was now convinced that Juan was not Juan. This was a trap. Chic asked himself, if he were setting this trap, how would he plan it? He worked out his next move based on what he thought would take place on the boat. Chic removed his Ka-Bar from his ankle scabbard and put it in his belt. He had already put his .38 under the left side of his belt. If he was wrong in what he was about to do, he would seek forgiveness later.

Chic approached the *Mermaid II* and hailed Juan: "Juan, Chic here. Are you ready?"

"You bet, man. Come aboard."

Chic did as he was told, looking as calm as possible. Chic approached Juan and put out his hand to introduce himself. When Juan took Chic's hand, Chic put a move on him, slamming him to the deck with the Ka-Bar on his throat and his knee in his belly, pinning his right hand to the deck. Chic made this maneuver where he was facing the door of the cabin. Chic felt he needed this guy alive to provide him information. He was of no value dead. If someone charged him from the cabin, whoever he was would be dead. Chic kept his eyes on the cabin as he removed his .38 from his belt.

"Quickly, your name!"

Georgie stared into Chic's eyes. Chic knew immediately this was not Juan. Chic knocked Georgie out with the butt of the Ka-Bar and in one fluid motion charged the door to the cabin.

Larry heard something hit the deck hard. By the time Larry peaked out one of the door slats, what he saw was a blur of Chic flying in his direction pointing his .38 at his head.

Larry fired three shot from his 9mm in the direction of Chic. One of his shots showered Chic's head with splinters, causing Chic to roll toward the bow of the boat. Chic recognized that the guy had the advantage with his 9mm.

Larry had never been in a gun battle, and when Chic fired a shot that hit a couple inches into the planking of the boat next to his head, he panicked. He quickly fired off several rounds in the general direction of Chic, causing him to duck behind the cabin. Chic glimpsed Larry as he jumped from the *Mermaid II*, headed away from the boat. Chic didn't have a good shot, but he took one anyway, hitting the windshield of the car next to Larry's head.

Larry ducked into a Mercedes sedan, speeding away from Chic. Chic fired a shot into the fake Juan's leg, hoping to keep him on board until he could return.

Larry took off in the direction of the waterfront. Chic was very familiar with Belize and immediately knew how to cut off Larry's escape. Chic knew from experience that a running gun battle was nothing new in Belize. They had walled off the old city, separating it from the tourist areas. This car chase was going to take place in the old city, based on the direction Larry was headed in, away from the boat.

Chic was able to get ahead of Larry and wait for him to come down the street. He only had to wait a few minutes before Larry came flying down the road toward him.

Chic rammed Larry's car in the left rear, causing him to crash into a power pole. While Chic's Ford was disabled, he was unhurt. Chic was waiting when Larry excited his car, firing his big 9mm wildly. Blood was flowing from Larry's head. Chic, hiding behind his open door, waited until he saw his opportunity. Larry turned to find a safer place to hide, but while turning, he exposed himself to Chic. Chic fired two shots, one hitting the heart area and the other into his head. Larry was dead by the time he hit the ground.

⚬────◆────⚬

Chic was faced with a large problem. Here he was in Belize, a foreign country, at the scene of two wrecked vehicles and Larry's body. On the fishing boat, *Mermaid II*, was the body of Juan and Georgie, who he shot in the leg. To his credit, he had proof of his association with the sheriff and police officers in Pensacola and Fort Walton. The sheriff of Escambia County had also notified the authorities in Belize that Chic was there on official business. Chic would soon find out how much water this would hold in Belize.

As the police approached the scene, Chic stood with his hands raised in the air. The pistol was on the car hood. Chic was handled like a stone-cold killer until the police were able to confirm who he was and why he was in Belize. Chic and the local authorities, after what seemed to be an eternity, returned to *Mermaid II* to retrieve the body. Fortunately, Georgie was still on board and alive, although he was in bad shape. He had lost a lot of blood from the gunshot. Juan's body was found, as expected, in a locker under the seats.

———•———•———•———

Roberto was in charge of *Angel* as it departed the dock at the cartel's resort. The Zeta cartel was in full attack mode against the Sinaloa cartel for killing their banker. They had developed good intel for this operation, up to a point.

What they didn't know was that the cartel and bankers didn't arrive at the same time or from the same point of origination. Otherwise, the Zeta plan of attack worked perfectly. A scuba diver had been dropped off and was waiting at a point where *Angel* would make a turn to starboard after leaving the dock to the open Caribbean. The diver knew that the bottom of the yacht would be examined immediately before its departure but not afterward.

As the yacht made a slow turn to starboard, clearing the island's inlet, the scuba diver approached on a motorized sled. The scuba diver attached two explosive packages to the yacht, one in fore and one in aft. He then moved into the Caribbean under the yacht, peeling off as he approached deeper water. The diver dropped to the bottom, allowing the yacht to gain separation. The scuba diver heard the yacht pick up speed. In this clear water, he was able to judge that the yacht was a safe distance away. He then made his way to a fishing boat trolling in the Caribbean.

He set the timer for twenty minutes. Zeta assumed all of the bankers and Sinaloa bosses would be aboard by then. The explosion was massive. Everyone on board was killed. There was little left for the investigators to examine.

***

It helped that two of the best men Belize City had on their police force were sent to Juan's boat. By the time they arrived, Georgie was awake and able to talk. Chic was allowed to participate in the investigation. As the officers were in the process of investigating Juan's boat, there was a very large explosion toward the sea. The reaction of the officers and Chic was to jump down into the boat, looking for cover. When it seemed safe, they stood and could see the massive plume of smoke seaward.

It was determined that Juan was killed with a puncture wound to the right temple. An ice pick, which was believed to be the instrument used to kill Juan, was found in a holster on Georgie's belt.

Georgie refused to confess to killing Juan, but he did spill the beans on Larry. There was no love lost between Georgie and Larry.

Chic picked up enough information about the explosion from police radio traffic to know that the yacht *Angel* had been blown up in some kind of terrorist attack and that all aboard the yacht had been killed. The names of the dead had not been disclosed.

The officers allowed Chic to secure his equipment, which was on Juan's boat, in a locker at police headquarters.

After around three hours of work in and around Juan's boat, and giving statements to the police, Chic was released to go with several officers to the cartel's resort in a police helicopter.

Chapter

19

The cartel had spared no expense in building a world-class resort. Chic was impressed.

"Hello, Mr. Chic. I've heard so much about you."

Chic turned to see a six-foot-one, well-built Belizean officer, about forty-five years of age, decked out in a sharp, well-starched police uniform and speaking as one fresh from Oxford University.

"My name is Captain Raintree. I'm in charge of this investigation. Come along. I'll bring you up to date on what we know. I understand you had a little excitement over in Belize City."

"Thanks for inviting me, Captain Raintree. I came here, as you know, to essentially spy on the cartel members who were on the yacht, *Angel*. I didn't have any real hope of gaining much useful information. I certainly didn't expect to witness the demise of the Boston end of this cartel. Do you know exactly who was on the yacht?"

"The best we can determine is that two bankers from Boston were on board along with one member of the Sinaloa group from Mexico City. Two more cartel members were to join the yacht while they were underway, but our information is they were not on board at the time of the explosion. Of course, everyone on board was killed. We may never have a true head count."

Chic looked around. There was very little confusion at the resort. Somebody had the employees under control.

"Captain Raintree, have you seen a young white woman here by the name of Myra? I have some unpleasant news for her. The man I had to kill is one of the Boston bankers and is Myra's boyfriend. Unless I can talk you into telling her the news, it seems like my burden. Captain, it might be helpful and safer to have you present. When she sees me come in, she'll know that Larry is dead. I have no idea how she will react."

"Absolutely, my good man." Captain Raintree always responded with an upbeat smile, flashing his white teeth. "Who knows, she may actually give us some useful information. We talked to her earlier. and basically she provided us no real information other than she was here as Larry's guest. Generally, the employees and guests who have given us statements have been very guarded in their comments. Perhaps you can open up the beautiful lips of this sexy-looking lass."

"Captain Raintree, I'll give it my best shot."

The two men found Myra sitting in a chair on the deck overlooking the Caribbean, with a pina colada in her hand. Myra actually was a good-looking woman. Chic could see how she could lead Larry around. When she saw Chic come through the door, it was as though she were immediately transformed into the personification of Medusa, the Greek goddess. Myra fit the description: a vile creature, roaming the earth with snakes as her hair, attempting to escape a living hell.

Had Chic's imagination gone wild? Chic blinked, and his vision adjusted to reveal a very real Myra, not the vision of Medusa.

Chic was confident that the vision of Myra as Medusa was a truer version of the real, live demonic creature occupying the body of this woman.

"Good afternoon, Myra. I hope you don't mind talking to me. I'm sure your family will want to hear that you're okay when I give them my final report on my investigation of Ken's death."

The look she gave Chic was pure evil. Medusa would have been forced to turn away.

Chic had pondered whether Myra would be embarrassed for her family to know the truth about her relationship with Ken's killers and how she profited from his death. Chic could see in her look that her real family now was the cartel. She would sacrifice her family on this altar. In fact, she had already sacrificed her brother.

Chic saw another thing in those evil eyes. Myra was ahead of him. She had already figured out that Chic was not going to tell her family anything about her secrets. Chic was too nice a guy to be the bearer of that kind of bad news. He was simply going to tell her mother that, based on his research, Ken was dead. So, Chic, in that short pause, decided not to press Myra.

"You know, Chic, this is really not a good time to talk about my family problems. A lot of people here have lost love ones on that yacht, so we need to respect their sorrow." Myra's concern came from her mouth like a flicking snake's tongue, searching for small prey.

"I heard you were here with a man called Larry, Myra. Was he on the yacht?" Chic had decided to play her game. Would she even admit that she knew Larry was dead?

"Yes, Chic, I was here with Larry. I have a personal life separate from my family. Larry was going to join the yacht later on a helicopter. We are certain he was not on the yacht at the time of the explosion. I'm sure he will find me a little later on today."

"Myra, do you know any of the people who left the resort on the yacht?"

"Not really. Larry had some friends on board, but I didn't actually meet any of them, so I'm really not of much help. We had only arrived from Cancun, so I didn't have a chance to meet anyone. That's all I can tell you, Chic. Now, if you talk to my mother, tell her I'm okay. I hope you will excuse me. I need to get in the sun and soak up some rays. Hope you don't mind."

"Nice talking to you, Myra. Hope you enjoy your stay here. If you hear from Larry, please let Captain Raintree know."

"Absolutely, Chic. I'll do that."

As Chic and Captain Raintree left Myra, Chic didn't know what Myra was really up to, but he firmly believed that her association with the Sinaloa cartel was just beginning to become serious.

Chic stayed in Belize for another three days working with the local authorities on the case. As he had suspected, the Boston bankers were all dead. The Mexican cartel was still intact, with only one member dead. The only connecting link was Myra, whose place in the cartel was unknown. The FBI was on the case. Chic was certain that BCWB was in serious trouble.

For all practical purposes, Chic had completed the job of dismantling the crime syndicate that had tried and failed to kill him and Suzy.

Several days later, Chic decided it was time for a psychological readjustment, which meant a slow sailboat trip to somewhere with Suzy. Chic was sitting alone at his favorite cantina on the west side of Isla Mujeres, sipping a drink made from passion fruit, when he placed the call to Suzy. Chic couldn't explain why a sailboat was the place he always returned to in order to gain his spiritual renewal and psychological balance. All that counted was that it worked.

As Chic prepared to dial Suzy's cell phone, the wait and the stress created by his battle with the cartel began to lift. The great weight of that moment became apparent. Surely the burden of waiting to hear from Chic on the outcome of this fight was even more critical to Suzy.

"Hey, babe. You ready for a little R&R?"

"You bet. What have you got in mind, sweetie?"

"How about a slow sailboat to Ft. Lauderdale? I can't make it to China, so hopefully Ft. Lauderdale will do."

"Sweetie, I thought that the hero always got on his horse and road off into the sunset. Whatever happened to that kind of ending?"

"You know I don't have a horse, but the main problem is that the cowboy rides off alone. I intend to go east with the real hero in this case."

"And who would that be?"

"Babe, that's you. If there is a hero in this case, I give that title to you. You earned it. Please get on the next flight out of Atlanta to Cancun. I'll be here waiting for you."

The following night, Chic and Suzy were well on their way to Dry Tortugas. The fifty-one-foot southwestern Hinckley rode the waves like a horse in stride making ten knots over the ground. They had been gone several hours when Chic's world phone rang. It was Heath.

"Chic, Heath here. I just received some news from the FBI. They called to let me know that at this point they do not have enough information to arrest Myra. They will continue to investigate her on tax evasion issues.

The agent asked me to inform you that the information you provided made it possible to continue the investigation, and he sends his sincere thanks. When you get back, he wants to meet with you as soon as possible."

"That's great news, Heath. I think we can all be happy we shot the demon between the eyes. I'll call you in a couple of weeks."

Chic was satisfied that the tide of evil that had almost killed both him and Suzy and that had brought terror to many innocent souls had crashed on the rocks of God's law. The demons had retreated to their dark lair, restoring harmony in God's infinite universe.

Chic and Suzy lay on the deck of the boat, hand in hand, taking in the unbelievable majesty of the heavenly sky, unspoiled by light pollution. The surface of the sea flashed with the bioluminescence of the sea creatures. The boat created no noise as it rode the waves and current in a following wind. The sensation gave them the illusion they were simply floating through the night sky as much a part of the universe as the stars themselves. As they entered that heavenly bondage of body and soul, their spirits soared freely with the angels.

Myra made her way to Cancun, and from there she flew to Miami. In Miami, she boarded a flight to Buenos Aires, Argentina, to meet with Jose Barbolla and Miguel Lazzino of the Sinaloa cartel. El Chapo Guzman had been transferred to the US federal prison system in New York. As far as Myra was concerned, he was already toast. From her experience in the drug cartel business, exposure to the public meant certain death. The infrastructure required to invest billions of dollars in a clandestine way was extensive. Notoriety was totally inconsistent with secrecy.

Myra leaned back in her first-class seat, sipped her Jack Daniels, and looked up at her seatmate, catching his eyes as they focused on her legs. Hungry eyes glazed over with visions of forbidden pleasure. Satisfied with her power over men, she relaxed into a semiconscious reverie. Knowing that a man she didn't know sat next to her who was consumed with lust aided this process.

New adventures lay ahead of her. One door closed, but another opened.

Myra knew the first time she met El Chapo that he lusted after her. She had full confidence that El Chapo made this meeting possible. Myra knew that she was going to discover who was the real boss of Sinaloa. Her plan was to bring Sinaloa into the modern world of money laundering. There was clearly a need. Greed insured that plenty of functionaries who had access to billions of dollars were ripe for the picking. Myra had the contacts. These dumb shits couldn't buy what she had. She, on the other hand, was for sale. More importantly, the Sinaloa cartel knew it was she who was responsible for her brother Ken's success. She designed the business plan now used by Sinaloa. Ken merely followed her plan. It was her plan that provided direction to the Sinaloa functionaries who actually controlled the flow of money to all of the underbosses.

Myra was the master of all she saw within her world vision. She relied upon the power of her mind and the attraction of her body, which were her primary tools. She could not explain how or why she was thrilled with her life. Was it the power, the danger, the greed, the control of her little world? She recognized that she loved to abuse men who responded to her animalistic scent as begging, submissive children, meekly whining to experience her sexual favors. This, along with the expectations of high-yield profits from her business acumen, made her irresistible.

As if from nowhere, a bright light flashed into her subconscious mind. Still semi-awake, a vision appeared—real or not, it seemed real. It was as if she had entered Dante's hell. She saw hell—Satan, his demons, all were there. She thought she may have seen Ken. She knew there was no hope for those who entered this world. Flee or enter the gates? She had now followed Lucifer to the gates of hell. As she entered, she willingly left behind any goodness that may have remained in her life. She grasped the hand of Lucifer. Myra morphed into her new state of being as Medusa.

> All we like sheep have gone astray; we have turned every one to his own way; and the Lord hath laid on him the iniquity of us all. (Isaiah 53:6)

> How art thou fallen from heaven, O Lucifer, son of the morning! *how* art thou cut down to the ground, which didst weaken the nations!

For thou hast said in thine heart, I will ascend into heaven,
I will exalt my throne above the stars of God: I will sit also
upon the mount of the congregation, in the sides of the
north. (Isaiah 14:12–13)

———•———•———•———

Chic was viewing the marvelous night sky.

"Love." Chic nudged Suzy. "Look at that sky. Have you ever thought of what it really means when we say God is the alpha and omega, the beginning and the end?"

"Yeah, sweetie, I have. I've decided that humans are not smart enough to actually understand eternity. We certainly can't understand the infinite."

"Absolutely right. The human race is in a way like Satan. We want to believe we can be as God. Within that desire, humans seek their own way, just as Lucifer did when he was cast from heaven. The battle between God and Satan began that day and will continue forever. For the same reason, our fight with crime will never end. It is the eternal battle between good and evil."

"Well, Chic, that's a depressing thought. But I am comforted when I think of Handel's *Messiah*. He began the story of Christ, the Prince of Peace, with the tenor aria, 'Comfort Ye My People.' Then he follows with a tenor aria, 'The Mountains Made Low and the Valleys Made High.' This is followed with a bass aria, 'The Refining Fire.' Certainly Handel is presenting the Prince of Peace in a prophetic way.

"A brilliant man was Handel! As I look at the stars, I'm reminded that God's universe is in a continuous process of creation through death and destruction. New life evolves out of destruction. In the human sphere, truth is light that will win over death or darkness. He brings victory over the grave."

"Tonight, Chic, God's peace will silence the demons. Come here. I need a kiss."

"Eight bells, all is well."

About the Author

Kenneth L. Funderburk graduated from Samford University, attended graduate school at Mississippi State and received his juris doctor degree from the University of Alabama. He has practiced law for over fifty years and is active in the art and music community. He is the senior partner in a law firm and has served as a County Attorney for many years. He has a wide business background including as a real estate developer, is on the board of several small businesses and was the founder and chairman of the board of a savings and loan. He is a member of the 10th Street Art Gallery, Columbus, Georgia and has won multiple blue ribbons in juried competition in the acrylic medium. He has served as part time choir director in churches in several states. Many of the events in the novel come from 20 years as Captain on his Amel 40' ketch yacht sailing the entire Caribbean Island basin. He has been involved in community service for his entire adult life.

CPSIA information can be obtained
at www.ICGtesting.com
Printed in the USA
JSHW080513230723
45234JS00003B/13